Cathy caught her breath on a gasp of sheer outrage. "I don't need your kind of help."

Anger still riding high in his eyes, Robyn countered, "You mean you don't *want* my kind of help. It's abundantly clear that you need help!"

"When I want anybody's help, I'll ask for it. Until then, I'll thank you to keep your opinions of my psychological hangups to yourself." Turning abruptly from him once more, she stumbled over a large root in the path and sprawled to the ground.

Robyn looked down at her, the faintest hint of a grin touching the corners of his mouth. "I would be a gentleman and offer to help you up, but I don't dare. A certain little spitfire told me I couldn't offer help until she asked for it."

"You—you—rotten man!" she exploded. "I'd lie here and die before I asked for your help!"

"I'm sorry. But you do matter to me, and I intend to help you whether you want it or not."

Dear Reader,

The Promise Romance™ you are about to read is a special kind of romance written with you in mind. It combines the thrill of newfound romance and the inspiration of a shared faith. By combining the two, we offer you an alternative to promiscuity and superficial relationships. Now you can read a romantic novel—with the romance left intact.

Promise Romances™ will introduce you to exciting places and to men and women very much involved in today's fast-paced world, yet searching for romance and love with commitment—for the fulfillment of love's promise. You will enjoy sharing their experiences. Most of all you will be uplifted by a romance that involves much more than physical attraction.

Welcome to the world of Promise Romance™— a special kind of place with a special kind of love.

Etta Wilson

Etta Wilson, Editor

Rainbow of Promise

Adell Harvey

Promise Romances™

Thomas Nelson Publishers • Nashville • Camden • New York

To my sister, Helen

Published in Nashville, Tennessee, by Thomas Nelson, Inc. and distributed in Canada by Lawson Falle, Ltd., Cambridge, Ontario.

Printed in the United States of America.

All of the characters and events in this book are fictitious. Any resemblance to actual persons, living or dead, or to actual events is purely coincidental.

Scripture quotations are from THE NEW KING JAMES VERSION. Copyright © 1979, 1980, 1982, Thomas Nelson, Inc., Publishers.

ISBN 0-8407-7362-5

Chapter One

Cathy jabbed her key into the lock and turned the knob. For the first time, she ignored the intriguing woven patterns on the thatched walls of the cottage. She was too intent on getting the baby out of the drenching rain.

The gusty New Guinea wind snatched the door out of her free hand and slammed it hard against the thatch. Not bothering to close it, she deposited Jed safely in his crib, then ran back out in the pounding downpour to carry five-year-old Heidi into the house.

With both children safe, she lit the kerosene lamp and breathed a sigh of thankfulness at being finally home. The Highlands Highway was treacherous even in dry weather, but during the heavy monsoon-like rains, navigating the slippery curves had taxed her endurance to the limit.

Cathy quickly changed Heidi and Jed into dry night clothes. Then she settled the sleepy children in bed for the night. She fixed a cup of coffee and sighed as its warmth relaxed her fingers and throat. It was good to be home. Her eyes took in the familiar room—crowded now with the children's beds, moved here temporarily from the main house. The wicker love seat was piled high with bright chintz pillows, and a straw mat served as a rug to mark off the conversation area from the kitchen. Quaint kerosene lamps shed a soft light, which reached to her own cot, standing at the other end of the long room. The restful avocado, mauve, and white color scheme suited her.

A smile played around her lips as she remembered her first reaction to Bonnie's suggestion that she come to Papua New Guinea with Bonnie and Joel to look after the kids while Joel worked on his doctorate in linguistics. The very name "New Guinea" had conjured up visions of mud huts, spear-toting cannibals, and frightening insects and snakes. But even as she had protested, Cathy suspected she would ultimately give in to Bonnie's persuasion. Didn't she always?

Ever since Bonnie's parents, the Jordans, had taken Cathy in as a foster child in her early teens, she had felt obligated to do whatever Bonnie asked. Spunky, vivacious Bonnie was always kind in her demands, more a benevolent dictator than a tyrant. But a dictator, nonetheless, Cathy thought ruefully.

She glanced at the clock on top of the kerosene refrigerator. Ten o'clock already! It had taken much longer to return from driving Bonnie and Joel upcountry than she had anticipated.

She rinsed the coffee cup at the tiny sink. It would be good to be alone for two weeks, just herself and the children, while Bonnie and Joel trekked into the interior villages taping syllables of native dialects. There would be no one around to hide from, no more pretenses, no sham—just two blissful weeks of letting down her hair and being herself, plain old Cathy Litton.

Plain old Cathy Litton? She glanced into the mirror and chuckled. With deft fingers she pulled the pins from her hair, already loosened and tousled by the wind, and shook it free from its tight chignon. The shining black tresses bounced lazily down her back. Enormous, dark-fringed green eyes smiled back at her from the mirror, no longer concealed by the wire-rimmed dark glasses she normally wore.

Reaching far back into the corrugated wardrobe, Cathy pulled out a lace-smothered filmy negligee. She slipped out of her jeans and man-tailored shirt, giving them a disgusted fling in the direction of the laundry hamper. She breathed deeply, enjoying the delicious feel of the soft, clingy material as it floated down over her body. The negligee, worn only when there was absolutely no possibility of being seen, was her one concession to her innate femininity and love of beauty.

Picking up a recent issue of *Vogue*—Bonnie's determined link with civilization—Cathy curled up in the wicker love seat. It was a night made for reading and relaxing.

The wind blew against the doors and windows, and whistled around roof corners and eaves. The sound of falling water was everywhere, streaming against the windowpanes, thudding on the roof, splashing off the porch. Just outside the window, a giant toad croaked his "humph-humph," an eerie sound in the blackness of the night's downpour. She was thankful for the sturdiness of the house against the fierce winds, and the screens against the determined insects which seemed to rule the tropics.

Cathy had only one complaint about life in the abandoned mining company quarters they were renting— the unremitting heat and humidity. There were no seasons and, therefore, no relief. Breakfast was greeted with a cheery eighty degrees on the thermometer, which steadily rose all day into the nineties, dropping back to eighty at nightfall. The unrelenting heat made life in New Guinea something of a marathon endurance test. It was tolerable only by frequent dips in the stream bubbling through the camp or the mining company's ingeniously designed outdoor showers.

The storm was growing worse, and Cathy became restless. She could hear the wild snapping of tree branches and the wind shrieking with greater intensity.

7

Maybe staying alone here was not such a good idea after all.

Nonsense, she told herself. They had been living at the mining camp for nearly six months and nothing had harmed them. She would go to bed—sleep would chase away her groundless fears. And after her long, grueling drive through the storm, she knew sleep would come easily.

As she rose from the settee, she froze, not breathing. The blur of white at the window behind the love seat had been—she was positive—a face! A white man's face.

She stood rigid for what seemed an eternity, unable to take her eyes from the window. She shivered slightly as she stood listening. There was no sound except the ominous roar of the wind and rain. And there was no movement behind the blur of water on the windowpane, nothing but blackness in the yard beyond.

She must have imagined those wild, staring eyes. Nobody would be out on a night like this, certainly not one of the natives from the nearest village. The nearest white men were the mine supervisors and engineers at least seventy-five miles farther inland, and missionaries on the interior stations miles away. None of them would be out in this storm, much less staring in her window.

Still, she found herself terribly shaken. Uneasily, she moved toward the door, intent on securing the deadbolt lock. She went rigid again as the door flung open, leaving her hand extended in mid-air.

A tall man stumbled into the room, drops of water glistening on his dark, curling hair. His drenched jeans and shirt clung to his lean muscular body. Blood trickled from a small gash in his forehead, marring a broad, square-chinned face. Wide-set eyes, glazed and blurred, yet blue as cornflowers, gazed at her helplessly.

"Accident," he murmured and tumbled awkwardly onto her bed.

Cathy ministered to the unconscious stranger, bathing and bandaging his wound, keeping cold cloths on his hot forehead. In an effort to stop his violent shivering, she removed his wet clothing, cringing all the while.

I'm becoming a regular little Florence Nightingale! Maybe I should have trained as a nurse or a nanny— it would be more practical than the degree I did get. Willfully, she stopped her bitter thoughts. An unbidden tear rolled down her deeply tanned face, and she hastily wiped it away. She had long ago stopped feeling sorry for herself and had no intention of starting again just because an injured man had tumbled in when she was tremendously tired.

She changed the cloth on the intruder's forehead, unconsciously brushing back a damp curl as she did so. A deep longing surged through her, and she pulled back as though she'd been burned by a hot torch. Cathy checked the bandage once more. Satisfied the bleeding had finally stopped, she burrowed into the pillows on the love seat and fell into an exhausted sleep.

Early dawn sunlight gilded the room, rousing her to wakefulness. Sleepily, she reached to pull back the mosquito netting, groping in vain for its familiar softness against her fingertips. Disoriented, she sat up and looked around. Memory returned as she saw the injured man tossing restlessly in her bed at the opposite end of the room.

She was startled to realize that she had spent an entire night alone in a room with a man without being overcome with fear. Resentful thoughts sprang up within her. There was a first time for everything! And the fact that he was wounded and helpless surely had something to do with her calm.

9

But he wouldn't remain weak and helpless. Hastily, she slipped into the kitchen area and dressed in her usual costume—baggy jeans, over-large plaid shirt, and sneakers.

She brushed and looped her long dark hair back from her face and twisted it into a tight knot at the nape of her neck. The severe style made her look older, less innocent, effectively hardening the wraith-like features of her oval face. Slipping on wire-framed dark glasses that effectively hid her amber-flecked avocado eyes, she looked at her reflection in the mirror and grimaced. There, that should do it.

Secure in the knowledge she was safely camouflaged, Cathy set about her normal morning chores, preparing to feed and dress the children. Two-year-old Jed was already gleefully bouncing up and down in his crib, rattling the safety rail. Cathy hugged the little boy to her, nuzzling her head in his tiny, baby-scented throat. "You darling," she cooed softly. "You're adorable....My own little Dutch boy."

As if in answer, Jed's tiny bow-shaped mouth burst into an impish grin, revealing deep dimples in each rosy cheek. He reached chubby arms toward her, and Cathy's heart lurched at his obvious affection. "Oh, if only you really were my own baby," she sighed.

Enough of this, she warned herself. *He isn't mine.* I might as well resign myself to second-hand love from other people's children. Fortified with a new wave of resolution, Cathy set Jed in the high chair and gave him a teething biscuit to pacify his hunger while she helped Heidi.

A puzzled Heidi stood in the middle of the room, pointing uncertainly at the sleeping man. "Who's that, Aunt Cathy?"

"Shh. He's…he's just a friend of your father's. He's sick, so be quiet and don't wake him. Come here and let me put this on you."

Heidi, independent as always, pulled away from her.

"No! Wanta dress myself!" Cathy usually delighted in Heidi's efforts at self-help, laughing silently at her inside-out blouses, misbuttoned closings, and backward boxer shorts. But the little girl's slowness aggravated her this morning. She felt an unconscious need to skip the play time, to hurry through the morning chores. Her sense of urgency continued while she fed the children, and Heidi was quick to pick up on her impatience. "Whatsamatter, Aunt Cathy?" she asked candidly. "Mommies are 'sposed to have the grumpies, but not aunts!"

Chagrined, Cathy hugged her tight. "Nothing's the matter, sweetheart. Aunt Cathy's just a little confused this morning." She took the children out to their fenced-in play-yard, entered the house, and tiptoed to the bed where the injured man lay, bending down to check the bandage on his forehead. She started when his hand shot out and covered hers. "I...I didn't mean to disturb you," she muttered stiffly.

He sat up, and the sheet fell away from his shoulder, revealing a chest tanned to the color of bronze. Unconsciously, Cathy stared at the muscular symmetry.

"Pretty good tan, huh?" he teased carelessly.

Cathy's face flushed deep crimson.

Amused, he offered his hand. "Since I've apparently made myself at home in your bed, I'd best introduce myself. Robyn Harroway, mining equipment field representative and recent accident victim."

Cathy shyly took his proffered hand. "Cathy Litton," she stammered.

Robyn glanced around the room. "I thought I heard children. Yours?"

"No...my niece and nephew."

Robyn fell silent momentarily, as if trying to remember something. "Then that ravishing beauty who took care of me last night must have been your sister?"

"Uh, yes," Cathy lied. So what if he guessed wrong? Bonnie wouldn't be back for two weeks and he would be long gone by then. Her camouflage was working.

"What happened to you?" she asked, changing the subject.

"This?" He reached up and patted his head. "My Jeep skidded off the highway last night in the storm and rolled down a small embankment. When I came to, I saw a light here and fought through the undergrowth until I stumbled into your door."

"Does it hurt much?"

Robyn shook his head. "Doesn't seem to, but I feel a little dizzy...probably a mild concussion."

"Maybe some hot tea and toast would help," she offered, heading for the kitchen end of the room.

As she arranged the tray, she was acutely aware of his keen eyes following her movements. His look made her jittery. Clumsily, she sloshed tea onto the toast when she set the tray on the small wicker table near the bedside.

He gazed at her intently. "Hey, calm down. I'm not going to bite you. In fact, I don't even bark very loud."

Cathy laughed nervously. Reaching out for her hand, Robyn continued to speak softly. "Look, I've guessed that we're here alone, but I can assure you I'm completely respectable."

She instinctively pulled back from his touch. "No man is completely respectable," she mocked bitterly.

Robyn pulled himself up, propped casually by his elbow. "What have we here? A man-hater?"

"You might say that."

"I might say it, but would it be true?"

Cathy shrugged. "Call it what you like. I just don't have a very high opinion of men."

He quirked one eyebrow, surprised at the vehemence of her outburst. "Sorry. I didn't mean to pry into your private affairs." Abruptly changing the subject, he asked softly, "Where's your sister this morning?"

Caught off guard, Cathy asked, "My sister?"

"The one who took care of me last night."

How stupid of me, Cathy chided herself. *I've got to be more careful.* Regaining her composure, she tried to cover her previous lie with a second one. "Oh, you mean Bonnie. She left early this morning for a trek...I mean, she'll be back this evening."

She turned away, unable to meet his steady gaze. Did he know she was lying? Thankful for the dark glasses that concealed the confusion in her own eyes, she shifted uncomfortably under his assessing look. She felt almost naked as his bright blue eyes ran slowly over her. His look unnerved her. He looked at her as if she were an attractive woman. Despite her efforts at concealment, the frankly admiring appraisal made her feel delicately feminine. And feeling feminine was something she must avoid at any cost! She tore away from his deliberate gaze. "I've got to check on the children," she murmured, hurrying from the room.

"Look at Jed, Aunt Cathy!" called Heidi.

"Oh no," Cathy groaned. Jed had found a mud puddle left over from the storm and was gleefully wallowing in it, sloshing mud from head to foot. "You don't look like my little Dutch boy now," she scolded softly, brushing mud from his straight yellow bangs. "A little more of this mud, and folks will think you're a native!"

She gingerly picked up the mud-caked toddler and carried him to the outdoor shower. Jed kicked and squirmed happily in the cool spray, and Cathy scolded, "Hold still! You're as hard to hold on to as a slippery greased pig!"

"Slippey pig!" Jed squealed with delight, squirming all the more.

"Hold still!" she demanded once more, trying to wash the mud off without getting herself wet.

Jed gave another mighty squeal and lunged toward her. Cathy's foot slipped, and she plunged directly under the shower spray.

Jed gurgled with pleasure, continuing to splash even more water on her. Heidi ran in to join the fray, giggling, "Oh, Aunt Cathy, you look so funny!"

A deep, masculine laugh interrupted the fun. "You do look funny," Robyn agreed from behind her.

Flustered, Cathy automatically reached up to secure her glasses. Where were they? Panic-stricken, she realized they had fallen off in the melee.

Robyn spotted the glasses just as she reached for them. Their hands touched, and their faces were mere inches apart. "Looking for these?" he asked as he held them up.

Cathy's eyes widened, and she gasped as he murmured huskily, "Your eyes are beautiful! They remind me of jade."

"May I have my glasses?" she pleaded, reaching in vain as he pulled them away from her grasp.

"Not yet. I want to look at your eyes. They seem so familiar...like the ones that haunted me in my sleep last night." He playfully put her glasses to his own eyes, then exclaimed in surprise, "These are nothing but colored glass! Why hide behind these ugly things?"

Cathy lowered her face to avoid his piercing gaze. "I need them for...for...because the glare hurts my eyes."

Robyn looked at her oddly. "There wasn't any glare in the house this morning."

"But, but...my eyes are weak...," she protested.

"Hey! I'm not going to hurt you. You look like a helpless, frightened fawn." His voice suddenly filled with compassion. "Here, let me help you out of this mess." He handed back the glasses and drew her to her feet, stumbling just a little from the physical exertion.

"Sorry," he muttered. "Guess I'm still weaker than I thought.

His superior height made her feel small and fragile, a rare sensation because of her own height. His touch on her wrist set her to shivering violently and she felt hysteria rising within her. The color drained from her face, leaving her chalk white. "Don't touch me," she whispered. "Don't ever touch me again."

Robyn drew back from her outburst. "You really meant it when you said you didn't like men."

"Did you think I didn't?" she asked sharply.

"Some men might consider that a challenge...like throwing down the gauntlet. An invitation even."

"Well, I'm sorry to disappoint you, but I'm not playing games. I'm the real thing...a man-hater."

Robyn studied the ground thoughtfully for a long moment. "Some man has hurt you terribly."

Cathy stiffened. "Men don't get close enough to me to cause pain. I neither like nor trust anybody of your sex!"

"Not even your own father?" he shot back.

Again, Cathy's face went white. "What gives you the right to intrude into my private life? To ask personal questions that have nothing to do with you? Now, if you'll excuse me, I've got work to do." She brushed past him angrily, slamming the door as she entered the house.

Chapter Two

Using the energy generated by her exploding frustration, Cathy went through the tiny house like a whirlwind. She changed beds, washed the linens, and cleaned the table, all but forgetting she had left the children alone in the yard with a total stranger.

Her energy spent, her emotions calmed, she ventured back outside to hang the clothes to dry. Robyn sat in the sandbox, entertaining the children with songs, stories, and sand castles.

Cathy smiled in spite of herself. "Aunt Cathy," Heidi called. "Come and listen! Robyn's teaching us funny songs!"

"I'm busy right now."

"Come on. Just one—just listen to me sing this one, okay?" Heidi begged.

With a sigh of resignation, Cathy walked toward the play-yard.

Heidi broke into a halting version of "Praise Him with the harp and lyre, praise Him with the tangerine..."

Robyn laughed softly. "That's tambourine, Heidi!"

Cathy raised an eyebrow. "Sunday school songs?"

"Why not? You know any better songs to teach them?"

"No, but…well, it just seems a little out of character."

"You mean the male of the species isn't supposed to know Sunday school songs?"

Cathy flushed. "I didn't say that."

"But you clearly implied it. Actually, you know little or nothing about my character." His gaze was directly on her again, his eyes unblinking.

Behind the safety of her stage glasses, she looked him steadily in the eye, willing herself not to be unnerved by the warmth of his look. This man was making her very uncomfortable, piercing through the iron facade she had so carefully and laboriously built around her emotions.

Without a word, she walked over to the clothes line where she self-consciously hung out the laundry, knowing those brilliant blue eyes were again following her every move. With relief she hung up the last dish towel and headed for the safety of the kitchen—out of range of those disturbing eyes.

Her thoughts were in turmoil as she prepared lunch for the children. She fluctuated between rage, terror, and dismay. How could she possibly get this man out of here? Injured, he was in no condition to hike back to the highway. And with no car, how could he travel the seventy-five miles to the mining headquarters? For her to drive him back was likewise out of the question. Travel alone with a man for that distance? Never! However, the alternative was equally unthinkable. There was no way he could stay here!

Drat him anyway! What right did he have to come stumbling in here, messing up her well-ordered life? The door burst open, and Cathy's eyes opened wide with amazement.

To the military chant of "Sound-Off," Robyn and the children marched in, wearing paper soldier hats and waving a white dish towel from the clothesline.

"What on earth?"

"We're trucing, Aunt Cathy," Heidi declared.

"Yeah, toocing," echoed Jed.

"You're what?"

Robyn grinned impishly. "We're calling a truce. This is our white flag, and we come with nothing but peaceful intentions. Besides, we're hungry."

Cathy's heart skipped a beat at his boyish humor. Despite her efforts to dislike him, Robyn had a devastating way of disarming her, of breaking through her cool facade. Though she deeply resented his intrusion into her life, she supposed she would have to make the best of it, at least for today. Only for today, she promised herself.

She sighed her capitulation. "Okay, lunch it is. But first, let's wash those dirty hands."

Lining up at the sink with Jed and Heidi, Robyn gave her an impish obedient-child look. "Yes, ma'am!"

Cathy felt the corners of her mouth quirk into a tiny smile, and fought it down. Life wasn't funny, and this mining engineer had no right making her think it was!

"For someone who is too badly injured to hike back up the road, you seem to have a good appetite," she observed as he served his plate with rice.

"Sitting out there in the shade with the kids revived me," he countered. "But only a little! I'm far from ready for the jungle marathon yet!"

Robyn and the children chatted gaily throughout lunch, and Cathy was amazed at how relaxed he was with them. The few fathers she knew certainly didn't waste time playing with children. Even Mr. Jordan, Bonnie's dad, had been gruff and uneasy around children, Cathy remembered. She would always be grateful to the Jordans for taking her in, and it was true they had treated her with love, but still, they weren't like a real family of her own.

"Penny for your thoughts," Robyn offered.

"They're not worth it," she assured him. "But I think it's time to put Jed down for a nap."

"Speaking of which, I'm a little tired myself. That blow on the head is catching up with me. Would you mind if I borrow your bed again?"

Cathy started to protest. "But..."

He touched his forefinger to her lips, a touch that sent her senses reeling in alarm. "Shh....no but's. If you can trust me for one more night, I thought maybe you could drive me up to pull out my Jeep tomorrow. Fair enough?"

Catching her hesitation, he tried another ploy. "I am at your mercy, you know. Surely you wouldn't throw a helpless, injured man out in the jungle, would you?"

Despite all her efforts to the contrary, Cathy laughed at his boyish pleading. "You win. I guess I couldn't live with that on my conscience."

He strolled to the cot, shoved the avocado netting aside carelessly and flopped down. "It's amazing what you've done with this room," he observed. "This cot looks like something out of the Arabian nights."

Cathy blushed with pleasure at the compliment, seeing the familiar room as it would look to a stranger. The cot, elaborately draped with the avocado netting and curtains, spread with an avocado and mauve striped quilt, did indeed look like an Arabian tent. The exposed plumbing pipes under the sink and lavatory glistened in the sunlight, the crinkled aluminum foil in which they were wrapped reflecting prisms of light.

Robyn's eyes followed her line of vision to the plumbing. "Ingenious idea," he admired. "Is this your handiwork or your sister's?"

"Mine," she admitted. "Actually, my sister and her husband live in the larger house across the play-yard. It just seems more convenient to have Jed and Heidi here with me while they're gone."

Robyn studied her thoughtfully. "Do you care for the children all the time?"

She gave him a wry look. "Let's just say most of the time. Bonnie and Joel are so wrapped up in their lin-

19

guistics work, sometimes I think they forget they have children."

"Lucky for them they've got you. But what do you get out of it?"

She didn't like the direction of his probing questions, not one bit. "I get to live in relative seclusion in exotic New Guinea!" she snapped. "I think you'd better rest now."

Almost as soon as she had so summarily dismissed him, Robyn was asleep. When Cathy finished putting Jed in his crib for a nap, she shot a glance at Robyn's quiet, sleeping form on her bed. Poor fellow, he really was exhausted. As if mesmerized by the steady rise and fall of his chest, Cathy continued to stare at the man who had managed to disrupt her life so completely in just a few hours' time. She had to admit he was very good looking, in a rugged sort of way. He had dark, shaggy eyebrows that almost met in the middle, framing those vivid cornflower eyes. His nose was prominent, yet suited his broad face and high cheekbones perfectly. His wavy dark hair was almost beautiful, yet completely masculine. But no matter how good looking he was, no matter how charming, no matter how apparently trustworthy, he was still male. As far as she was concerned, that was enough to make him persona non grata in her house. Her foster father had taught her no man could be trusted. Some of them were simply more obvious with their intentions than others. Robyn, apparently, was one of the more subtle ones.

"Let's play beauty shop, Aunt Cathy." Heidi's plea brought her back to the present. Cathy's hand shot up to her severe chignon, which Heidi was already beginning to loosen.

"Not now, Heidi," she protested.

The little girl was persistent. "But you always play beauty shop with me while Jed's asleep."

"Oh, all right. But this time I'll be the beautician and you have to be the customer."

Momentarily satisfied, Heidi sat down on the wicker stool in front of Cathy. "I think I'd like an elephunt style today," she said with an important air.

"Elephant style?"

"Yes, you know, fancy."

Cathy stifled a giggle. "You mean elegant, don't you?" With practiced fingers, she twisted and braided Heidi's long silky hair into elaborate French braids. "There. Does that suit you?"

Heidi peered into the mirror. "Simply elephunt—I mean elegant."

Cathy swatted her affectionately on the rump. "For someone whose parents are linguists, you sure murder the king's English!"

"Now I wanta do yours," Heidi insisted, pushing Cathy toward the stool.

"Not today, Heidi..."

Heidi started to pout. "Wanta do yours!"

Knowing she would wake Jed with her wails, Cathy surrendered. "Okay, you little blackmailer. But only for a few minutes."

With delight, Heidi loosened the thick black coils, brushing each strand ferociously.

"Ouch!" Cathy yelped. "Take it easy on my scalp, sweetheart."

"You have some bad brambles."

"Brambles? You mean tangles?"

Heidi turned abruptly toward the kitchenette. "I smell smoke..." Cathy jumped to her feet and ran to the kerosene refrigerator. Black smoke billowed from its chimney. "Oh, drat! I forgot to clean the wicks and chimneys this morning!"

She quickly turned off the flame and prepared to clean up the mess. Soot trailed up the walls and ceiling and clung to the curtains.

"So this is the simple, uncomplicated life in New Guinea," Robyn remarked laconically from behind her.

Cathy grimaced. "If an intruder hadn't barged in here unannounced, I would have remembered I needed to clean the chimneys and wicks today."

"Well, then, since I seem to be responsible for the mess, I guess it's only fair that I clean it up," he offered.

A feeling of chagrin hit Cathy. Just because she didn't like men was no reason to be such a shrew. "I'm sorry," she murmured, her eyes avoiding his. "It's just that I thought I finally had this cantankerous thing mastered. It took me forever to get the flame set just right so I wouldn't freeze the lettuce or thaw the meat. After a few messes like this, I learned that keeping a rigid maintenance schedule was the only way to avoid massive cleanups."

Robyn was already swabbing the walls with sudsy water. "Well, praise the Lord anyhow!" he exclaimed.

Cathy's eyebrows shot upward. "Praise the Lord anyhow? What kind of crazy talk is that?"

"It's not crazy talk. The Bible says to thank the Lord for everything. I guess that includes sooty messes."

Cathy worked silently for a few minutes, then asked abruptly, "Are you one of those Jesus freaks or something?"

"I must be an 'or something,'" he teased. "Because I'm not sure what a Jesus freak is."

"You know—one of those people who go around spouting scripture all the time."

Robyn thought that one over. "Maybe I am one, then. But I don't spout scripture all the time—I don't know enough of it yet."

Cathy's mouth formed a perfect little "Oh." Silently they worked side by side, scrubbing the soot off everything. When Robyn tiredly pulled out a chair to rest, Cathy was instantly contrite. "Oh, I forgot about your injury!"

"It's okay, just ran out of steam a little quicker than usual." He tossed her a flippant smile. "But don't get your hopes up…I need to stay here and rest more than ever now!"

A few minutes later, he effortlessly started the gasoline engine on the wringer washer so she could wash the curtains. Cathy looked at him in amazement. "You handle that thing like a pro."

He laughed. "Lots of experience. I help Marva Ellis with hers all the time."

"Marva Ellis?"

"You don't know the Ellises?" It was Robyn's turn to be surprised. "They're the Bible translators up the way in the Bsorio village. As the only other Americans around, I figured you would surely know them."

"They must be the ones Bonnie and Joel visited some time back. They mentioned an American missionary couple who were doing linguistic work near here."

"Your sister went to visit fellow Americans and didn't take you along?" The look Robyn gave her was one of incredulity. "Are you a total recluse here?"

Cathy felt her resentment rising. "I stayed here by choice to take care of Jed and Heidi—not that it's any concern of yours."

Undaunted by the chill in her voice, Robyn protested, "But the Ellises have three kids who would have been delighted to play with Jed and Heidi. Who are you hiding from?"

"I'm not hiding…" Cathy's voice trailed off, and a tear left a tiny white trail on her soot-smudged cheek. "If you must know, I wasn't invited to go with them."

Robyn was instantly by her side, tenderly brushing the tear stains away with his thumb. "You haven't been away from this place since you came, have you?"

Cathy's pent-up emotions, suddenly released by the first human kindness she had received in months, threatened to engulf her in tears. "I'm all right, honestly," she protested, trying hard to rebuild her defenses. "Just leave me alone."

"Leave you alone? It seems to me you've been left alone far too much already. What kind of sister would bring you to an isolated spot in New Guinea, dump her kids off on you, and expect you to do all the work?"

"It's not like that. Bonnie is just a little thoughtless, that's all."

Robyn was gazing at her intently, giving her that assessing look that made her feel so uncomfortable. Her hand went automatically to the nape of her neck to check the chignon. "Oh dear, my hair…Heidi let it down…" Flustered, she began a frantic search for her hairpins.

Robyn caught her wrist, pulling her toward him. He ran his free hand through the clouds of dark hair that curled around her face in the humidity. "With your hair down like that, you look exactly like your sister."

Caught off guard again, Cathy spluttered, "But Bonnie's blonde!"

"That conk on the head didn't affect me that much," Robyn insisted. "Your sister was a ravishing brunette—the most beautiful creature I've ever seen!"

Cathy flushed crimson. Trying to stammer a reply, she choked on the words.

Robyn continued to stare at her intently, while she avoided his gaze. She was already unnerved, and those piercing blue eyes had a way of seeing right through her. Suddenly he reached out and took off her glasses, holding her at arm's length while he studied her features.

"Let me go!" she insisted, struggling to be free of his iron grip on her wrist.

" 'Oh, what a tangled web we weave, when first we practice to deceive,'" he quoted softly. "There was no sister here last night, was there?"

Cathy couldn't force herself to look into his eyes. "No," she finally admitted. "I took care of you last night."

"But why the masquerade?"

"I was afraid…"

"But I was dazed and exhausted from beating through the jungle in the storm. I couldn't have hurt you."

This conversation had gone far enough. "If you'll give me back my glasses, I think I'd better get these curtains hung out on the line," she said, breaking free at last from his grip.

Robyn's eyes met hers with a pleading look. "Please trust me. I want to help."

"I told you—I'll never trust any man!" she snapped.

"Well, then at least believe that I won't hurt you. Please don't be afraid of me."

"I'm not the slightest bit afraid of any of your species."

Robyn's look mocked her. "Then you won't be needing these to hide behind, will you?" He thrust the glasses into his shirt pocket.

"I told you, I'm not hiding!"

"Oh? Then why the ugly clothes and the old maid hairdo?"

Cathy was indignant. "Who gave you the right to assess my clothes and hair?" she fumed. "I'll dress the way I please!"

"If that's the way you please, fine. But somehow, I get the feeling you don't like the uglies either."

"It's none of your business!" she seethed. "I'm sorry if my ugliness offends you. I suppose you think you're an Adonis—God's gift to all of us poor, male-starved women!"

"No, on the contrary, I never quite considered myself a lady's man," he answered thoughtfully. "But neither did I say you were ugly. I just can't understand why someone so outrageously beautiful would deliberately try to hide that beauty."

The amber in her eyes deepened, flashing her dislike with hard, golden flints. "As I said before, how I

25

dress is none of your business. Now, I'd like to hang out these curtains." She picked up the laundry basket and strode past him with an air of angry determination.

Momentarily defeated, Robyn moved aside. "Fine. I'll grab a drum of kerosene and get this refrigerator back in gear."

Cathy attacked the curtains like an angry lioness. In her fury, she snapped several clothespins. *Calm down*, she chided herself. But how could she? No man had ever broken through the shell she had so carefully erected around her emotions. *Then along comes this Robyn, this Jesus freak*, she thought indignantly, *and pitches life into utter turmoil*.

"Does Joel have any spare drums of kerosene stashed away someplace?" At the sound of Robyn's voice, Cathy jumped.

"Sorry, I didn't mean to startle you," he continued. "But all your kerosene drums are empty."

Cathy looked bewildered. "But Joel promised to have them filled before they left."

"Looks like he forgot. Oh well, they'll be back tonight. I guess the food won't spoil that quickly."

Cathy shot him a puzzled glance. "Tonight?"

Robyn frowned. "You said your sister was returning tonight, didn't you? Or was that more of your little masquerade game?"

Cathy flushed and lowered her eyes. "Actually, they won't be back for two weeks."

His eyes widened in disbelief. "Two weeks?" he exploded. "What sort of man would leave you alone here for two weeks with his kids, and not even leave proper supplies?"

Cathy shrugged helplessly. "Joel isn't a bad sort, as men go," she added meaningfully. "But he's so wrapped up in his work, he tends to forget little details."

"Little details?" Robyn flung the words in disgust.

"And how do you propose to keep Jed's milk cold, your lamps lit—you call those little details?"

"I'm not exactly helpless. I've got the radio, and I managed quite well before you arrived. I'm sure I'll handle things equally well when you leave tomorrow!"

"Well, I don't intend to leave you without kerosene! Go pack up the kids and get in the car," he ordered.

Cathy was so startled by his command she automatically began to comply. Halfway into the house, she turned and called, "Where are we going?"

"Up the Highlands Highway to the Kapalis," he answered matter-of-factly.

"The Kapalis?"

"Yes. Kesena Kapali has a gas station in his backyard. It's where the Ellises get their fuel oil."

While Cathy piled Jed and Heidi into the Land Rover and buckled their seat belts, Robyn loaded two empty kerosene drums into the back of the vehicle. Surprised by her own compliance with Robyn's demands, Cathy pondered the situation. What was there about this man that irked her so, yet at the same time charmed her so much she would unquestioningly obey him? And, despite all her efforts to the contrary, she found herself beginning to trust him—even to relax a little in his presence.

"You'd better drive," he suggested. "Give me a chance to rest."

Chapter Three

The Highlands Highway was a long grey ribbon snaking through exuberant vegetation. Lofty trees adorned with ferns, orchids, and mosses stretched sunward, and strangler figs wrapped other, less fortunate trees in fatal embraces. Cathy bemoaned the occasional clear-cut tracts which marred the scenery, but Robyn assured her they would soon be overgrown with thick, second-growth brush.

About fifteen miles up the road they were halted suddenly by the New Guinea version of a flagman, a toothless, shirtless native waving a large red stop sign. When the Rover came to a halt, the flagman simply pointed to a yellow construction sign at the side of the road.

"*Wok Long Rot. Ol Kar Mas Stop*," Robyn read. "Understand it?"

Cathy studied the sign. "Work along road. All cars must stop?"

He smiled his admiration. "That was great! You *tok pisin* pretty good!"

"*Tok pisin?*"

"Talk pidgin," he translated.

"Not really," she admitted. "It was just a lucky guess. Bonnie and Joel are the only linguists in the family."

As they sat and waited for the construction workers to clear the road, she found herself chatting about Heidi's hilarious language lapses, the pidgin language, and life in New Guinea.

"Aunt Cathy," Heidi interrupted. "We're getting hungry."

Cathy glanced at her watch, then at the rapidly descending dusk. "Good grief! Have we sat here that long?" she exclaimed in dismay.

As if in answer, the road crew parked their equipment directly across the road, effectively barring any passage. They began to pick up their tools, as if closing down for the night.

Robyn got out to investigate. After talking to one of the men, he came back to the car and shrugged. "Seems it's quitting time, and the road isn't repaired. We can't get through until morning."

Cathy looked worriedly at the gas gauge. She had failed to get gas during the rain storm last night. There certainly wasn't enough left to drive all the way home and back up to the station again.

"Not enough petrol, huh?" Robyn observed. He studied her intently. "May I offer a suggestion?"

"I suppose anything is better than sitting here in the middle of the road all night. What are our options?"

"The road to the Ellises' village is just a way back. We could go visit them until the road is fixed."

Cathy hesitated. "But wouldn't they mind? I mean, we just can't drop in on somebody and spend the night."

"This is New Guinea, not Philadelphia," he said laconically. "Most missionaries are delighted to have fellow countrymen drop by. The welcome mat is always out at the Ellises."

As they sped back through the forest, Cathy stole quick glances at her passenger. His clipped accent had puzzled her from the first.

"Are you British?" she asked abruptly.

Robyn turned in the seat. "No Aussie."

"Australian? I didn't think you sounded like an American."

A shadow crossed his face. "Ah, yes, Australian through and through."

"You don't sound very pleased about it."

He fell silent, seeming to concentrate on the coffee plantations they were passing. "I'm proud to be an Aussie," he said finally. "It was the station I needed to get away from. Being constantly reminded that I was born solely to carry on the Harroway family name, to manage the family property..."

Cathy was instantly sympathetic. "So you became a mine equipment representative to get away and do your own thing, right?"

Robyn gave her a brooding look. "You do understand, don't you?"

The Bsorio village, set among plantations of shiny-leafed coffee trees, consisted of two rows of low, circular huts separated by a long strip of bare earth. Smoke seeped through the roof thatch of the picturesque houses, whose walls were intricately woven in various designs.

Captivated by the village landscape, Cathy exclaimed, "It's enchanting! Just like a travel brochure."

"The enchantment stops here," Robyn warned her as she cut off the ignition and helped the children out. "Inside the huts are dark and unventilated, filled with smoke and animal dung."

As if to prove his point, pigs, chickens, and an emaciated little dog wandered in and out of a nearby hut at will. The bare strip between the huts, still damp from last night's rain, was smeared with pig droppings and red splotches from chewed betel nuts.

A winsome child—clad only in the leaf apron which covered his buttocks—sat on a log, throwing *kaukau* peelings to a pet hornbill bird. In the middle of the clearing, an old man squatted zombie-like, his face and naked body painted in mourning with yellow-green mud.

Instinctively, Cathy drew the children closer to her. Noticing her movement, Robyn hastened to reassure her. "There's no danger. Despite their fierce looks, the Bsorios are very even tempered and gracious. The kids are probably safer here than they would be in Chicago or New York."

"Uncle Rob! Uncle Rob!" Three tawny-haired youngsters descended on them gleefully, broke through the darker-skinned Bsorios milling about and reached up to hug Robyn's long, lean frame. He affectionately ruffled their curls, encircling all three simultaneously.

"Keith, Karl, and Kara Ellis, this is Cathy Litton and Jed and Heidi Rogers," he announced formally.

The tall, gangly Kara, who looked to be nine or ten years old, stood back and eyed Cathy carefully. "So you finally found a girl friend," she announced. "I guess she'll do, but her face is awful dirty!"

Cathy's hands flew up to her face in alarm. Good grief! She had forgotten to wash the soot off! "Why didn't you tell me?" she demanded of Robyn. "I must look a fright!"

"I never noticed. You look beautiful to me."

The familiar flush appeared on Cathy's soot-smudged cheeks. What was happening to her? Normally, a little soot on her face wouldn't have mattered to her at all.

As if reading her thoughts, Robyn remarked, "It's a good sign."

"What's a good sign?"

"The fact that you're concerned about your appearance. For a while there, I thought you deliberately wanted to look as unattractive as possible."

Cathy ignored the comment and rummaged through Jed's diaper bag for a Wet 'n Dry. Hastily she scrubbed her face with the astringent, then pulled her hair back

31

with a rubber band. "There. Does that suit me better?"

Robyn frowned. "No, it doesn't suit you at all!"

Her insolent glare was interrupted by the arrival of Marva and Pete Ellis. "Robyn, nice to see you. And who's the lovely lady?"

As Robyn completed the introductions, Cathy grimaced. *Lovely lady in a pig's eye*, she thought ruefully. But what did he know? Stuck out here wasting his life trying to change the traditions of the natives, he probably hadn't seen another white woman except his wife for months.

Robyn explained their problem, and just as he had predicted, Marva graciously insisted they stay the night. "It won't be any trouble at all," she assured them. "It will be a delight to have guests."

"'Fraid you won't get much sleep, though," Pete warned. "Tonight's the Bsorio singsing and the festivities will go on all night." Nodding toward Jed and Heidi, he added, "I hope the children aren't light sleepers."

Cathy laughed. "Are you kidding? A hurricane couldn't keep those two awake."

They walked over to the Ellises' home, an intricately woven thatch hut similar to the others in the village, but much cleaner, Cathy noted. A delicious aroma filled the air as they went inside, and Pete ushered them to seats at a crude, handmade dining table. While they talked, Marva dished up steaming mugs of the local staple, sweet potato soup with green beans, onions, and a little meat. The talk turned immediately to linguistics, and Cathy discovered the Ellises were in the village as language learners. It was their job to listen closely to the language, then attempt to write the sounds phonetically.

"After our work is finished," Pete explained, "the real linguists come in and develop an alphabet, enabling the Bsorios to have a written language. Next, the people are taught to read their language. And finally, the Bible translators come in, giving them the scriptures in their own tongue."

"But is all that really necessary?" Cathy asked. "Most of them talk pidgin."

Pete nodded. "That's what we used to think, until we visited the Ngaing tribe about two hundred miles from here. The pastor read a scripture passage in pidgin, then asked if one of the villagers could translate it into their own tongue. Not one of them could."

"Pidgin is basically a trade language," Marva cut in. "And it's very difficult to express theological terms or abstract thoughts like love, joy, and peace."

Robyn laughed. "Tell her how hard it was to translate snow into something New Guineans could understand."

Pete explained, "In Isaiah 1:18 the Bible says, 'though your sins be as scarlet, they shall be white as snow...' Trouble was, few natives have ever seen snow. The *tok pisin* word '*sno*' means mist, which is a dirty grey color."

"So," Marva added, "the translators came up with '*waitpela olsen ais*'—white as ice—the white stuff commonly seen in the freezer sections at the larger food stores."

"I can see it would be difficult," Cathy admitted. "But is it really important for them to have the Bible? They've had their own culture and religion for centuries. Why should we force ours on them?"

There was a stunned silence in the room. Finally, Pete replied, "No one is forcing anything on anyone. We're simply trying to show them the way of salvation—God's way."

"I don't mean to be rude," Cathy said. "But it just seems if their way of salvation, as you call it, has satisfied them for generations, why isn't it good enough now? The anthropologists say it's a great disservice when we try to mold everyone into our ideas of civilization, destroying their tribal identities."

Robyn looked at her oddly. "Do you think these people are really happy, with their human sacrifices, body-scarring rituals, and self-torture to appease the spirits?"

Cathy shrugged. "And who's to say we civilized mortals with our stained glass windows and ornate sanctuaries are happy?"

"No one is truly happy without the Savior," Pete answered quietly. "Regardless of nationality, civilized or not."

Marva broke the uncomfortable tension. "Rob, why don't you take Cathy out and show her the village? Pete and I will look after the kids and clear up these dishes."

"This your first singsing?" Robyn asked as he piloted Cathy through the crowd, holding lightly to her elbow.

Cathy's gaze swept around the crowd. Natives in every imaginable type of dress crowded the village, many of them trying to jam into a forty-by-eighty foot spirit house on the ridge top.

Robyn made another attempt at conversation, raising his voice above the din of the singing and tribal dancing. "Did Bonnie and Joel ever bring you to one of these?"

Cathy shook her head. "They went to a few of them, but I stayed home to look after the kids."

"It figures."

"Why are you so intent on making them look bad?" Cathy demanded.

"I just think they take advantage of you, that's all. If you were my sister, I'd at least take you around to see the sights."

Seizing the opportunity to change the subject, Cathy asked, "Do you have a sister?"

"Three of them—which presents the problem," he

answered. "As the only male Harroway, it's up to me to furnish some Harroway sons." Robyn looked thoughtful. "Dad has never let up trying to get me married off."

Cathy's mouth quirked with humor. "Is the prospect of marriage that frightening?"

"Not marriage per se. But I would like to do my own choosing. Dad has had it in his mind for years that a certain neighbor's daughter would be a good match for me, thereby joining our two spreads in the bonds of unholy matrimony."

The glum look on his face warned Cathy it was no laughing matter, so she refrained from making a wise crack. "But how about you?" Robyn was saying. "Why aren't you married and tending your own children instead of over here raising someone else's?"

She stiffened. "Man-haters don't marry," she said harshly. "And speaking of the children, I'd best get back to them."

Robyn caught her arm. "The children are fine. Marva promised to look after them so we could enjoy the evening. So enjoy."

Ignoring Robyn completely, she turned her attention to the sights around her. It seemed the men had tried to outdo each other in their traditional finery. Bird-of-paradise feathers adorned elaborate headdresses, pig-tooth necklaces, conch shells, or ropes of beads hung around their necks, and all of them had quills or tusks pierced through their noses.

Some of the men wielded feather-and-flower-decorated machetes, while others slung carryall *bilum* bags over their shoulders. Bright headbands, some of woven feathers, others of strung beans, seemed to be the style of the day, many sporting large white medallions in the center of the forehead.

"Creative lot, aren't they?" Robyn observed, following her line of vision from one gaily bedecked native to another.

"Typical males," Cathy retorted. "Always strutting around like peacocks."

Robyn swung her around to face him. "Are we that egotistical? Do you think I'm such a show-off?"

Cathy averted her eyes. "Well, maybe not that bad," she admitted. "But you do have an air of assurance about you, as though you expect every woman who looks at you to be attracted to you."

He caught her hair loosely in his hand, tilting her head back to look up at him. Grinning down at her, he murmured, "Are you attracted to me?"

Her breath caught in her throat at the insolence of his question. "I asked you once before never to touch me," she seethed between clenched teeth.

Robyn only grinned bigger. "That didn't answer my question, but I'll speak for myself. I do feel attracted to you—very attracted."

Without warning, his lips were on hers, gently coaxing for a response. Hysteria rose within her. When she at last struggled free of his embrace, her eyes were deep green smudges of pain in her pale face. Rubbing her hand across her mouth as if trying to erase his touch, she screamed at him, "I hate you! I hate you!" She turned and ran toward the Ellises' home, where she threw herself on the cot in the guest room, a hunched-up ball of misery.

"Cathy?" Marva's tentative call roused her to reality.

"Come on in," she sniffed, not wanting company, but not wanting to be rude to her hostess either.

Marva gave the door a tiny push and hurried to her side. "What happened to upset you so? Did one of the natives frighten you?"

Cathy swallowed hard. "He…he kissed me!" She shuddered at the memory of it, once again feeling those gentle, warm lips on hers.

"Robyn kissed you? But why the terror? Lots of men

36

have been known to kiss pretty girls," Marva chided lightly.

"But you don't understand. No one has ever kissed me…" She could feel the walls crumbling, something she couldn't allow to happen. Coldly, she said, "If you don't mind, I'd rather not talk about it."

Marva looked hurt. "It's all right. But if I can help…"

"No one can help," Cathy blurted with an air of desolation. Sensing her abject misery, Marva sat back down on the cot. "I don't want to pry, but I do want to help, Cathy. Try me."

Cathy sat up, searching Marva's features as if looking for a glimmer of understanding from the older woman, some evidence that she could be trusted. "I just feel sick and angry at Robyn for daring to kiss me."

"Is that all he did—one kiss?"

Cathy glared at her. "Isn't that enough?"

Marva was bewildered. "But if it was only a kiss …surely you've been kissed before."

"Never!" Cathy sizzled. "I don't want men slobbering on me! Oh, I hate him!"

"You hate Robyn? He's always seemed like such a nice fellow. The children love him."

"No, I don't hate Robyn!" Cathy sobbed. "It's my…my…" She nearly choked on the words.

"Who do you hate, dear?" Marva prodded gently.

"My foster father." The words came out in a hoarse whisper.

Marva gulped. "Your foster father?"

Cathy fidgeted with her handkerchief, reliving the terrible memories. "Not Mr. Jordan. I only went to live with them after…after…." She struggled for control of her emotions. "After I was a teenager," she finished lamely.

As understanding of Cathy's tragic past burned into her, Marva said gently, "I see."

Her defenses cracked at last, Cathy flew into an uncontrollable rage. "No, you don't see! There's no way you can know the humiliation, the fear, the...."

Deep sobs shuddered through her body as she relived the horrors of her youth. Marva sat quietly, simply rubbing her back and trying to help her through the violence of her released emotions. When the storm had subsided somewhat, Marva consoled, "But that's all in the past, Cathy. You can't let it ruin your entire life."

"It has already ruined my life," Cathy sobbed bitterly. "I'm terrified of men. None of them can be trusted...they only want one thing from a woman...."

Marva smiled. "Now, that's not entirely true. I happen to know a number of trustworthy fellows. Saint Paul says we should forget those things which are behind...."

"Don't start spouting scripture at me," Cathy warned. "I tried the religion bit when I went to the Jordans, but it doesn't help."

"Maybe you should have tried Christ," Marva reprimanded gently. "There is a difference between religion and knowing Jesus Christ personally."

A questioning look played across Cathy's face. "You're talking Greek."

Marva started for the door. "Another time, then. Meanwhile, why don't you get some rest? I'll tend the children if they're restless during the night."

Her ragged, pent-up emotions spent, Cathy lay back on the small bed—drained, yet oddly relaxed. It was good to be able to talk to someone at last. And no children to worry about for an entire night!

She was soon fast asleep, impervious to the wild music and dancing that went on all night.

Chapter Four

The arrival of dawn rescued the village from the all-night onslaught of the singsing. After the constant pounding of drums and dancing feet, the village seemed eerily quiet.

Cathy wakened to Jed's loud whine, "Want Aunt Cathy! Want Aunt Cathy!"

She hurriedly dressed and went into the kitchen, hesitating at the door for fear of facing Robyn after last night's incident. But she found Marva alone with the five children, valiantly trying to get them all fed. Chagrin surged over her. "Oh, I'm sorry. I shouldn't have slept so late. Here, let me help."

With a skill born of much experience, she soon had Jed and Heidi under control and offered to feed one of Marva's toddlers.

"You handle those kids like a pro," Marva observed. "Been tending them long?"

Cathy brushed a loose hair back into her chignon. "Ever since they were born. Kids make Bonnie nervous."

"Bonnie?"

"Bonnie Rogers, my foster sister."

"Oh, yes, we had them here one afternoon," Marva remembered. "The young couple working on a doctorate in linguistics."

Cathy nodded. "With seven hundred different dialects here, Joel figured New Guinea was the best place to study. It's a ready-made speech laboratory."

"Don't I know it," Marva joked. "Just listening to one tribe here makes my head spin. Just when I think I've got their syllables mastered, some motor-mouth lets off a whole string of new ones!"

She began to clear the tables, and Cathy looked around questioningly. "Have the men already eaten?"

"Oh, I meant to tell you," Marva explained. "Pete and Rob left early this morning to see if they could get Rob's car out of the ditch with our truck. Rob said to tell you he'd get the kerosene, too. He thought you might prefer to stay here and rest."

Cathy scraped the plate in her hand with a vicious motion. "That's just a polite way of saying he didn't want my company!"

A smile pulled at the corners of Marva's mouth. "Perhaps he thought you wouldn't enjoy his."

Cathy's flushed face was the only indication she had heard the remark. Marva glanced out the window. "Whoops! My customers are lining up already. Would you mind stacking the rest of the dishes while I go to work?"

"Customers?"

"Patients. Pete and I do dental work and run an emergency clinic here on our front porch."

Cathy shot her a puzzled look. "I didn't know you were doctors."

"We're not. We both took emergency technique and jungle medicine training before coming here. And in my pre-missionary days, I was a dental technician." She shrugged. "We're not the most qualified medical team in the world, but we're all the Bsorios have."

Cathy sent the children out to play and soon had the kitchen sparkling clean. Wandering out to the front porch, she watched in amazement as Marva efficiently tended one patient after another.

A young man dressed in a calf-length wrap-around skirt was seated on a folding chair. His eyes were closed tightly in pain. A friend stood behind him, clasping his forehead with both hands so he couldn't move his head. Marva worked inside his clamped-open mouth and soon held up the offending tooth for all to see. The man rubbed his jaw, swilled the antiseptic she gave him, and grinned weakly. The ordeal was over.

Next in the chair was an elderly native with a badly ulcerated leg. Cathy's stomach did flipflops as she watched Marva bathe the wound, then swab it with sulphurdine on a cotton swab.

Marva glanced up at her pale, chalky face. "If this one bothered you, you'd best not stay around for the next patient," she warned.

But it was too late. A teenager, perhaps thirteen years old, stumbled up to the porch, obviously in great pain. His head was shaved bald, and at first glance, Cathy could see nothing physically amiss. However, when he turned around to take the chair, Cathy nearly fainted. His back was a bloody mass of oozing sores that looked like raw hamburger.

"Torture scarring by the witch doctor," Marva explained, already at work cleansing and disinfecting the boy's back. "They worship the alligator god and start mutilating their backs at an early age so their scarring will look like the alligator's rough skin. They believe they can't make it to paradise unless they look like the alligator when they die." Marva couldn't resist one little dig. "It's this kind of thing that makes us disagree with your anthropologist friends who want to preserve native traditions."

Cathy gulped. "I think I'll check on the kids."

She found them under a coconut palm, where Heidi was trying to teach them her new songs. "But they already know all my songs, Aunt Cathy," she pouted. "They said they taught them to Robyn!"

"We did!" Kara insisted. "Uncle Rob didn't even know Jesus when he first came here, but we taught him!"

Cathy let that news soak in for a moment. So Rob learned religion here from the missionaries. She laughed at the irony of it. They came to save the illiterate natives and caught a well-educated Australian instead! She left the children to their own devices and strolled around the village. *Might as well see what there is to see of New Guinea while I have the chance*, she thought absently.

A group of natives were gathered in the clearing, pointing and gesticulating furiously. One held a small slate. As Cathy drew closer, she realized the village court was in session. She stayed to watch the proceedings, catching a word or phrase of pidgin occasionally. It appeared from the gestures that the young man on the stand had been seeing someone else's wife.

"Figures," Cathy muttered. "Even native males can't be trusted."

The next offender was accused of working witchcraft against another clan. Both men paid a fine and the slate was wiped clean.

She hurried back to the house and prepared lunch while Marva finished up with her patients. She found herself eagerly looking forward to adult conversation. Alone with Jed and Heidi so much, she hadn't realized how desperately lonely she had been. Oh sure, Bonnie and Joel talked to her when they were home, but they were so involved in each other and with their work, she usually felt like a fifth wheel in their presence.

Happily she chatted with Marva, sharing the results of the village court. "They made a big production of cleaning the slate each time," she said.

Marva chuckled. "That's another one you can chalk up to the Bible translators. Trying to explain how Jesus forgives our sins and washes away every stain, a missionary picked up a slate and washed it off," she explained. "Many of the tribes caught the concept, and now use it to show a man's crimes are paid for, and he starts over with a clean slate."

Cathy toyed with the food on her plate. "Jesus doesn't forgive every sin, does he?"

"Absolutely. There's no sin his blood doesn't cover."

To relieve the silence that followed, Marva moved to the window. "We may get another downpour this evening. What say we take the brood down now for their baths?"

"Sounds good," Cathy agreed. "But don't you have more patients?"

"No, I doubt if anyone else will come in. The sing-sing will continue tonight, so the men will be busy sacrificing pigs this afternoon."

Rounding up the bath supplies and the children, Cathy could hear the terrible squealing of pigs. As they walked through the village toward the river path, she pulled Heidi and Jed close to her, trying to block their vision. The villagers were beating three large pigs on the head and chest with huge clubs, sacrificing them to the spirits.

Maybe some traditions need to be changed, she thought wryly.

It was a long, sweaty, twenty-minute walk to the water's edge, a fact which made Cathy especially grateful for the showers and stream back at the abandoned mining camp. When she voiced her thoughts to Marva, the missionary simply smiled. "The miners always have it easier than the missionaries in these places."

"But it hardly seems fair," Cathy protested. "Why can't you have a few conveniences, too?"

"We have plenty," Marva assured her. "But it's important that we live as much like the villagers as possible if we hope to win them for Christ. But what about you? You must have made some sacrifices to come out here to help your sister. Wasn't that out of love, too?"

The women were seated on the pole bridge that served as a walkway across the stream watching the children splashing happily. Cathy pulled her sneakers off and dangled her bare feet in the refreshing water. "Actually, I came because I felt I owed it to Bonnie. Her folks took me in after...after...." Her voice faltered and she looked away momentarily.

"But you don't owe her your life."

"Well, it couldn't have been easy on her having to share everything with me. And her folks were awfully good to me. Besides, I love...." Her voice broke again.

Marva glanced toward Heidi and Jed. "You wanted to stay with them?"

Cathy nodded. "I've never admitted this to another person, and I don't honestly know why I'm confiding in you, but I love children. Being a sort of pseudo-mother is better than nothing."

"But why...?"

Suddenly Cathy stood up. "Are we going to bathe, too, or waste our time talking all afternoon?" She pulled off her jeans and plunged into the water.

Walking back up the wet mossy trail was more difficult than going down had been. "By the time we get back to the top, I'll need another bath!" Cathy complained.

Marva laughed. "You get used to it!"

Robyn and Pete were waiting for them at the top of the ridge. Unable to face Rob, Cathy pretended to be engrossed with Heidi and Jed and began to chat nervously with the children.

"Slow down," Marva whispered. "You're running off at the mouth like one of my motor-mouthed natives!"

Robyn came toward her. "Looks like we have to stay here one more night so Pete can help me get the crazy Jeep back in shape. We had to tow it all the way here."

"I'm perfectly capable of driving myself and the

44

children home," she retorted. "You can stay here as long as you like."

"What? And leave you alone down there with that monstrous refrigerator? Nothing doing." Winking at Pete, he teased, "Convince her the wilds of New Guinea is no place for a woman to be alone, Pete!"

Pete looked uncomfortable. "Far be it from me to take sides in a domestic squabble, but I do think it would be better for Robyn to go with you."

Cathy's eyes flashed hard, golden flints. "Doesn't it ever occur to you male chauvinists that some of us women prefer to be alone?"

Robyn raised his arms in mock despair. "What do you do with an obstinate female?"

Pete laughed. "Marva and I will take the kids on home while you two argue it out in private, okay?"

Cathy looked quickly from one to the other, her objection obvious to all. Marva hugged her shoulders. "It's all right, Cathy. Honest."

As Pete and Marva and the children moved off toward the house, Robyn pulled her gently down beside him on a huge rock outcropping, reaching for her tinted glasses at the same time. "If we're going to talk man-to-man, I need to see your eyes." Cathy trembled violently as his hands brushed her face.

"You're just plain scared of me, aren't you?"

Her downswept long lashes effectively hid the fright in her eyes, but she nodded.

Robyn cupped her chin in his hand, tilting her face upward. "Please don't be frightened of me," he pleaded. "I'm truly sorry about last night. I don't know what came over me—I'm not in the habit of kissing women uninvited."

Color rising in her pale cheeks as she remembered his kiss, Cathy sat numbly. How could she respond when he was dragging her forcibly out of the painless limbo she had maintained for the past few years! He

45

was making her feel again, painful feelings that could only hurt and destroy her.

His rough hand ever so gently traced a tear streak on her cheek. "That mask of yours slips away every now and then, doesn't it?" he asked softly.

She gritted her teeth, steeling herself against his touch, her face full of revulsion. "Don't flinch," he pleaded. "I just touched you, nothing else. I promise I'll never try to kiss you again. Uninvited, that is," he added meaningfully.

Her eyes sparkled angrily. "You won't ever get an invitation from me."

Robyn tried once more to break down her defenses. "Look, I know you've been terribly hurt, but...."

"What do you mean?" she demanded, her voice full of suspicion.

"Well, Marva told me..."

Cathy was incredulous. "Marva told you about my family? How could she? I trusted her!" She began to sob hysterically. She felt utterly betrayed again, just as she had when her foster mother had railed against her.

Robyn sat helplessly by her side, while the great heaving sobs racked her body. Finally, as the sobs subsided he tried to comfort her. "Marva didn't say anything about your family. She didn't betray any confidences at all. She simply told me to be gentle with you because you had been badly hurt. And I think I had already sensed that anyway."

Cathy held her face in her hands. "So now you know the sordid story of my life," she said bitterly.

"I know nothing of the sort. All I know is you're an astonishingly beautiful person who has been badly hurt, who has built a wall around her emotions to escape from life."

Cathy turned her back toward him, unable to cope with the tenderness in his eyes. "I don't want to feel those emotions. Can't you understand that?"

He spun her around with both hands on her shoulders, and she cringed from the determination she could see in his face. "But you *are* going to feel again!" he promised. "I'm personally going to ensure it!"

That night, lying back on the guest room cot, Cathy dropped the book she had been trying to read. Her thoughts continually drifted to things she would rather forget. Painful thoughts. Ugly thoughts.

She lay awake a long time, staring at the moths playing in the moonstreaks on the ceiling, listening to the din of the drums at the singing.

No matter how much she resented Robyn's unwelcome intrusion into her affairs, she had to admit he stirred her long-dormant emotions. In all these years she hadn't cried one time, not over anything. And now, during the few days Robyn had disrupted her life, she was an emotional basket case, crying and whimpering like a baby.

What was it about him that disrupted her cynical view of life? Was it his gentleness, his apparent sincerity? Whatever it was, she could certainly do without it. She had come to terms with the circumstances of her life, had learned to ignore the hurt and humiliation, and was doing nicely. In the morning she would tell Robyn politely, but firmly, to butt out! On that determined note, she fell asleep.

By the time Cathy awoke, Robyn had already fed Heidi and Jed. They were serving as "fetch and carriers" while he and Pete worked on the Jeep.

"Look, Aunt Cathy," Heidi called proudly. "We're helping Robyn fix his car!"

"Yeah, heppin," Jed echoed, toting a ballpeen hammer to where Robyn lay on a mechanic's sled under the vehicle.

Robyn slid out from under the Jeep, wiping grease on an old rag. His teeth gleaming white against his grease-smeared face, he grinned broadly at Cathy.

47

"Good morning, sleepyhead. The drummers keep you awake last night?"

Cathy's heart lurched at the tone of his voice. What was there about this man that stirred her so? "Yes, the singsing was a little noisy," she lied, not willing to admit that thoughts of him had kept her awake most of the night.

"Well, just another hour's work on old Leaping Lena here, and I'll get you back home where it's quiet," he promised.

Cathy swallowed hard. Resolutions were more easily made in the dark privacy of her room than carried out in the bustling activity of daylight, she thought ruefully. Now was the time to tell him, to be firm. "I think it would be best for me to take the children and go now," she began primly. "You seem to have recuperated from the accident, and I'm sure you need to be going back to the mine."

Robyn quirked an eyebrow, his eyes twinkling. "Just like that—you're throwing me out, huh?"

Thankful for the dark glasses that prevented his reading the uncertainty in her own eyes, Cathy tried again for firmness. "If that's what you choose to call it, yes, I am throwing you out."

Instantly, Heidi and Jed were upon her, protesting vehemently. "No! We need Robyn!" Heidi wailed.

Robyn wrapped an arm around each howling youngster and grinned triumphantly. "See? The vote is three to one—a clear majority!"

"But, but…" Cathy faltered. "It's impossible…"

"Not impossible. Highly beneficial to us both, I'd say."

"Beneficial?"

Robyn measured his words, as if he had given the matter much consideration. "The engineering work I'm doing is on some of the cleanup operations at the old mine just up the road from your place. If I rent one of the empty houses by your sister's at the compound, it will save me a seventy-five-mile daily drive and enable me to keep an eye on you and the kids at the same time."

Cathy stiffened. "I don't need anyone to keep an eye on me!"

Robyn shrugged. "So, let's just say the advantages are all mine, then. But since we're going to be neighbors, we might as well be friends."

Still unwilling to admit defeat, Cathy ignored his out-thrust hand. "I may not be able to choose my neighbors, but I do reserve the right to pick my friends. And you'll never be among them; you can count on that!"

To her annoyance, Robyn simply grinned. "Well, the Good Book says to love your enemies, so if we're destined to be enemies, I guess I'll just have to keep on loving you!" He gave her a quick, playful hug with one arm and climbed back under the Jeep.

Cathy stalked into the house. She hastily bade her farewells to Marva and Pete, and loaded the protesting children into her Land Rover. "Wanna stay with Robyn!" Heidi wailed.

"Wanna stay!" howled her Little Sir Echo.

Angrily, Cathy swatted both children lightly on their seats. "No! We've got to leave now!"

Shocked by the unaccustomed scolding, Heidi and Jed hushed and looked at her accusingly through tear-brimmed eyes.

Cathy's anger simmered throughout the long drive home and boiled again when she tried to wrestle a bulky kerosene barrel from the Land Rover. Trying to fill the refrigerator from the kerosene drum was even more awkward. She broke several fingernails in the process, dropped the funnel twice, and splashed the acrid liquid on the floor. Finally, she flung the offending funnel across the room. "I hate them all!" she raged. "I hate Chester for ruining my life! I hate Joel for bringing me here! I hate Robyn for...for...I just hate him!" With each new flood of anger, she pounded her fist into a chintz pillow from the love seat.

In the midst of her rage, Robyn quietly opened the door. "Need some help in here?" he asked innocently.

She hurled the pillow at him. "No, I don't need any help," she sobbed. "Get out of here and leave me alone!"

Effectively ducking the pillow, Robyn shot her a grin. "Wow! This looks like all-out war. But can we call a truce long enough for me to get the refrigerator started?" Without waiting for an answer, he retrieved the funnel from the floor and soon had the refrigerator back in operation.

Cathy watched glumly as he took the kerosene pressure lamp off its hook, filled it, and replaced the cap. Next, he filled the preheating cup with alcohol, lit it, and waited for it to heat. When the alcohol was nearly gone, he unscrewed the pump and pumped vigorously, screwed the pump tight again, and finally turned on the lamp, then rehung it on the hook.

"Thanks," Cathy muttered.

"And now, after all my hard work, surely the lady will invite me for supper?" he teased.

"Sure, why not?" she shrugged. "Isn't there also something in your Bible that says 'If your enemy hungers, feed him'?"

The blue eyes that looked into hers were alive with understanding and tenderness. "We don't have to be enemies, you know." He moved ever so slightly toward her, and she trembled noticeably.

"I don't want you to touch me," she pleaded hoarsely, her eyes huge and intense.

She was so close to him, she could see the faint stubble of beard standing out against the bronze of his skin, the precise cut of his well-defined mouth. His dark hair, crisp and wind-tousled, curled around the neckline of his blue denim bush shirt. She was afraid

50

of this man, afraid of the feelings he provoked deep within her, afraid of the places her thoughts of him took her.

He stood silently, his eyes touching every part of her. "You're a strange woman. I still haven't figured you out."

His blue eyes flicked her face, her hair, her trembling body once more. She had drawn her hair back into its tight Grecian knot, but in the humidity, a few stray tendrils had escaped to curl beguilingly around her tear-dampened cheeks. His voice sank into a husky tenderness. "You're as beautiful as a princess," he murmured. "And I've always wanted to know a princess!"

"Well, don't suppose princesses have an easy life!" she retorted. Her hand went to her forehead.

His voice suddenly becoming thick with compassion, he reached for the aspirin bottle from the shelf above the kitchen counter. "You've had a rough, rough day. A couple of aspirin might make life a little easier, at least for today."

She gratefully reached for the tablets and glass of water he offered her, but as his hand brushed hers, she drew back in alarm.

He pulled back abruptly, his black eyebrows drawing together "What sort of brute do you think I am? Anyone would think I was about to beat you or drag you off someplace."

Quick tears sprang into her eyes. "I'm sorry," she said simply. She turned away from him, determined to overcome this weakness she felt in his presence.

Cathy put a hand to the loose tendrils of hair, poking them back into their tight confinement. She turned back to him, confident she was once more in control of the situation.

She was unprepared for the slightly mocking expression in his eyes, the barely noticeable upturn of his lips. "On second thought," he teased, "it might be safer for us to remain enemies. I'm not sure I would know how to handle a romance with a princess."

He lifted his head and smiled at her. She could feel her heart beating rapidly, her breasts rising and falling in agitation. She knew he could see his effect on her, the unbidden feelings he was arousing. She bit her lip, hard. She had to get control of herself; she must! As though poised for flight, she turned toward the door. "I'd better get the kids in for supper," she said quickly.

Chapter Five

Robyn managed to make the evening meal a delightful time. Laughing and joking with the children, he quickly had Cathy at ease.

"It's a marvel what you can produce from cans," he commented. "Who would have thought we could be eating canned bacon and eggs?"

"And spinach," Cathy noted, glancing meaningfully at the untouched portion of greens on Heidi's plate.

"Ah, yes, spinach!" Robyn exulted, with an exaggerated air. "Better eat your spinach, Heidi, so you'll grow big and strong like Popeye, the Sailor Man!"

"Who's Popeye?"

Cathy's eyes twinkled at the blank look on Heidi's face. "Someone who lived in comic books long before your time. Uncle Rob's age is showing."

Robyn opened his eyes wide in mock horror. "Don't tell me I'm experiencing a generation gap with a five-year-old! 'Who's Popeye?' she says. Why, he's only the greatest, strongest sailor who ever lived." He turned all his attention upon Heidi. "And he got that way because he always ate his spinach. So eat up."

Placing his arm casually over the back of Heidi's chair, Robyn put his face down close to hers. "Won't you do it for Uncle Rob? I thought you were my girl. All my girls eat their spinach!"

Cathy's face froze. "Heidi isn't any man's little girl," she declared icily.

There were several seconds of charged silence as Robyn's eyes narrowed on her in sharp question.

Disquieted by his blunt gaze, Cathy ordered brusquely, "I think you'd better leave now."

It was a dismissal that couldn't be ignored. Robyn started helplessly toward the door, stopping midway across the tiny room. "But...I was only trying to help."

"That kind of help we can do without. Now, please leave!"

His eyes flashed hard blue glints. "Okay, I'll leave. But I'd at least like to know what I said or did to provoke such a storm. How can I apologize if I don't even know what I did to offend?"

"I didn't ask for an apology—only your departure."

"I knew you were all strung out on those kids, but I certainly didn't think you were so hung up on your own importance you can't stand to see someone else helping them!" He threw a parting shot over his shoulder as he went out, slamming the door, hard.

Listening to his angry footsteps echoing across the porch floor, Cathy winced. Is that what he thought? That she was angry at him for trying to help with the children? Anger and resentment surged through her. Was it always going to be like this? Would she go through life making a complete fool of herself, blowing up at seemingly innocent statements, unable to explain her unreasonable reactions to apparently normal situations?

To staunch the scalding tears, Cathy turned to her usual means of emotional release. She tackled the cleanup tasks, almost violently stacking and washing the dishes, sweeping the crumbs from under Jed's highchair, and getting the children to bed.

With her emotional storm finally subdued, she wandered out into the bright moonlight of the early evening, past the children's play-yard, over to the stream that wound through the camp. Slowly, she followed the bubbling creek upstream, listening to its music as it spilled over boulders and around smaller rocks.

The sound of splashing water increased in intensity as she neared her favorite haven, a spot she had privately named Rainbow Falls. Often she came here with her problems, her heartaches. Somehow, watching the water tumble over the rocky incline calmed her nerves, helped her sort out her feelings. At certain times in the early morning when the bright sun streaked through the trees and played against the misting waters, she saw an ethereal rainbow effect. At these times, Cathy allowed herself to drop her hard, cynical veneer and to dream. Dreams of love and romance. Dreams which could never be a reality in her life.

But there were no rainbows tonight, and no dreams. She sat miserably on the mossy bank, letting the quiet dark beauty of the place penetrate her soul. A slight breeze stirred in the trees overhead, pulling at the stray strands of hair now free from the tight rubber-band. With one quick motion, Cathy released the band, loosing a cascading tangle of thick, raven curls. It tumbled around her shoulders, in stunning contrast to the yellow and green plaid shirt which so effectively hid her feminine curves.

She sighed deeply. Picking up a bamboo twig, she broke it into tiny bits and tossed the pieces idly into the rushing water. She watched as the pieces joined the current and moved away with gathering speed.

One of the larger bamboo twigs caught her eye. The water had washed it up onto a large flat rock, halting its forward movement toward the sea. Unexplainably, she felt a sudden rush of kinship with the tiny piece of debris lying on the moonlit rock. Pulling off her shoes, she entered the cold stream near the rock and released the twig, sending it once more on its way.

Wish someone would do that for me, she thought ruefully as she sat on the rock and dangled her feet in the cool water. She shook her head angrily. Ever since Robyn had appeared at her window, her thoughts had been topsy-turvy. Why had he come along and messed up everything for her?

The loud snapping of jungle undergrowth startled her. "Who's there?"

A tall, rugged form emerged from the dusky forest, stopping directly in front of her on the creek bank. "Would you believe it's David Livingstone?" Robyn joked, his voice determinedly light-hearted.

"I came out here for some privacy," she said, her voice cold. "Why did you follow me?"

"I was worried about you. I saw you leave the camp an hour ago. Somehow, it didn't fit your image for you to leave the children alone so long."

"An hour?" She was immediately abashed. "I had no idea. I thought I had only been here a few minutes." She jumped down from the rock, grabbing for her shoes. "I've got to get back to the kids."

Robyn stood in the path, effectively blocking her escape. "The kids are fine. I checked them just a few minutes ago. Sit down and relax."

Relax? With her heart pounding like a sledgehammer against her breast? "Let me go," she demanded. "I've been out here long enough."

He caught her hands in his and pulled her down to sit on the bank. The breeze ruffled the thick dark hair growing crisply away from his forehead, making him look very young and vulnerable. Cathy looked away. *Why, he looks like a helpless little boy*, she thought absently.

A faint narrowing of his gaze, a gleam entering his eyes that Cathy didn't understand, quickly changed her mind. She didn't like that look at all. She thrust her chin forward at a defiant angle and rose to her feet.

The oversize shirt, the baggy jeans, and her bare feet combined to make her figure shapelessly slender.

"You have the hardest shell I've ever seen," he commented dryly as he stood beside her.

Still avoiding his gaze, she countered angrily, "How do you know it's a shell?"

"Because every once in a while your mask slips, revealing a real flesh and blood female under all those tough defenses."

"There's nothing wrong with the way I dress."

Robyn's manner changed suddenly, as if he were tired of sparring. "You would look great in anything. But I came out here to apologize for hurting you at supper this evening."

Her defenses momentarily down, she asked in surprise, "Hurting me?"

"Yes. Something I did certainly bothered you deeply. And I know it had nothing to do with my getting Heidi to eat her spinach."

Cathy lowered her eyes. "It did and it didn't. Mostly, I was angry at myself for getting angry."

"I think that statement needs explaining."

She shrugged. "Sometimes little things trigger bad memories and I go off on an angry tangent. I get over it eventually."

He gave her a searching look. "You were forced to eat spinach as a little girl?"

"I wish it were that simple. The spinach had nothing to do with it." She unconsciously flipped her hair with her hand. "It's not important. Just forget it."

"Yes, it is important," he insisted. "Tell me about your parents."

Tension crackled through her. "Nothing to tell," she mumbled. "I never knew my parents, who they were, or are. I'm one of those homeless nonpersons, a product of the foster home system." The words were almost spat out, the bitterness reverberating through every syllable.

57

"Tossed from pillar to post, huh? One foster home after another?"

"I should have been so lucky," she answered sadly. "I went to my first foster home when I was just a baby, and there I stayed until...until..."

Robyn swatted at a mosquito, tactfully ignoring the tears in her eyes, the break in her voice. When she had regained her composure, he asked sympathetically, "Were they terribly mean to you?"

"Mean? Oh, no! I wanted so badly to be loved, to belong, I did anything 'Papa' asked me to. I ate my spinach so I could be 'his good little girl.' " She defiantly looked into Robyn's clear, blue eyes. "But being 'Papa's good little girl' entailed much more than simply eating my spinach...." Her voice broke once more, and she looked quickly away from his penetrating gaze.

Tiny dark flecks in his eyes smoldered alertly as his gaze swept over her features. He said nothing, but Cathy sensed a warmth of understanding, of compassion. She felt her protective armor crumbling, a harsh, shattering sound deep within her. Desperately, she fought for control. No matter how hard she attempted to deny it, the fact remained she was vulnerable, frighteningly vulnerable.

"I'm going back to the house now," she declared emphatically, a declaration that brooked no opposition. Resolutely, she turned and rushed down the path, back toward the mining camp.

Chapter Six

By morning, Cathy's defensive shell was back in place. She might have to put up with Robyn as a neighbor, but she certainly didn't have to tell him any more about her past! She would avoid him as much as possible, keeping a safe distance.

She glanced out the window toward the house he had commandeered for use. Avoiding him today wouldn't be difficult. His Jeep was gone from its parking place, signaling he had left for the mine already. She fought down the disappointment she felt rising within her. She was glad he was gone for the day. Glad, glad, glad!

As the day progressed, however, she found herself gazing across the camp with alarming frequency, listening for the sound of Robyn's Jeep.

The lowering evening sun cast its long rays into the forest shadows. A refreshing breeze lifted her free-swinging curls and tickled the tiny hairs on her arms. With much greater care than usual, she had brushed out the long locks, even brushed a tiny bit of mascara on her long lashes. Not even to herself would she admit she had spent more time on her grooming today, tucking in her shirt, revealing the softly feminine curves of her body.

Hearing the sound of a vehicle on the highway

above the camp, Cathy hurried inside her house and busied herself with supper preparations. When Robyn honked the horn loudly, she forced herself to stay indoors, ignoring his summons.

"Uncle Rob's home, Aunt Cathy!" Heidi called. "Hurry up. He's brought someone with him!"

Just what I need, she thought angrily. *More neighbors!*

Robyn appeared in the doorway, grinning broadly. "I sensed you were afraid to stay alone here with me, so I brought us some company." He motioned toward the drive, where a tremendous commotion could be heard.

Cathy ran to the porch. "What on earth?"

A native couple, their golden brown skin gleaming above their *asgras*, were unloading two squealing, wriggling pigs from the back of Robyn's Jeep.

Robyn smiled sheepishly. "Sorry about the pigs, but we'll fence in your garden right away so they won't root up your tubers! Come on out and meet your new neighbors."

The natives looked up from their pig-corralling efforts as Cathy and Robyn approached. *"Apinun, missus,"* they greeted cordially.

"Good afternoon," Cathy said, returning their pidgin greeting in English. Robyn performed the introductions in a curious mixture of English, pidgin, and Bsorio. "Foroba and his wife, Bate."

Cathy acknowledged the introductions as graciously as possible under the circumstances, and watched as Foroba and Robyn quickly erected a fence from sharpened casuarina stakes around her small vegetable garden.

"Wouldn't it be simpler to fence in the pigs?" she wondered aloud.

Robyn glanced up from his work, amusement written on his face. "No self-respecting native would ever fence in his pigs. A man's prestige depends on his ability to take good care of his pigs, letting them roam freely."

Cathy looked skeptical. "But don't they run away?"

"On the contrary. They forage freely all day, then return to their owner's house at night for food scraps. The men lock the pigs up only at night."

Again, Cathy raised her eyebrows, looking in the direction of Robyn's rented house. "And where do you presume to lock them up?"

"Over there." He gestured to another empty mining house. "Foroba will sleep in my place, and Bate gets the inner rooms of that house. The pigs will sleep in the outer room."

"You've got to be kidding," she protested.

"Nope. It's the way they do things around here. Men and women never sleep in the same house. The women get to sleep with the man's other possessions, namely, his pigs!"

Cathy shuddered. "Just like a man...thinks he can own a woman!"

"But the men take good care of them both."

The intimate, intense look he gave her seemed to curl her toes inside her sneakers. His gaze roamed over the classic beauty of her features, taking in her high cheekbones, the oval of her face, and the finely chiseled point of her chin. It came to rest on her eyes, eyes that seemed alive with golden glints reflecting the last rays of the setting sun.

"You look nice tonight," he observed, his glance traveling down to the cotton shirt she had tucked into her belt.

Cathy stared intently at the ground. Somehow he had uncovered a weakness in her protective shield, a weakness she wouldn't dare admit. "One intruder in this camp was bad enough. Why did you have to bring two more?" She nodded impatiently toward the newcomers.

"I happened to invite them for merciful reasons. It

61

seems Foroba has been accused of practicing witch-craft against a Gimi villager, and the Gimis demanded revenge."

"I thought revenge killings were ruled out around here."

"They were. But the Gimis insisted on a pig pay-ment. Foroba had just paid all his pigs but two for Bate's bride-price. If he gives up his final two pigs, he'll be reduced to nothing. In tribal culture, he will be considered an absolutely worthless individual, los-ing his self-esteem and his manhood."

"That's utter nonsense!"

"Nonsense to you, but a matter of life or death to Foroba. Anyway, I brought them here where the Gimis can't find him. They'll think he's run off into the bush somewhere and will spend a few days trying to hunt him down."

"But you can't hide them forever," Cathy protested.

Robyn shrugged. "After a few days some other ex-citement will capture their attention, and they'll forget all about poor old Foroba. Or if the man he sup-posedly made sick gets well, he'll be off the hook."

Cathy still wasn't satisfied. "But what if the Gimis come here looking for them? Are you going to leave us alone with them while you go off to the mine?"

He gave her a long, searching look. "Do you honest-ly believe I would have brought them here if there were any danger to you and the kids? Foroba's sorcery hearing was inconclusive. Somebody accused him of giving an old man a bad case of yaws. A couple of Mar-va's penicillin injections will have him as good as new in short order."

"But what am I supposed to do with them all day while you're gone?" she persisted.

"They won't bother you. Bate will keep busy with her pigs, and Foroba will hunt and fish, the usual man-type things. You may even discover you enjoy their company."

Cathy looked doubtful. "Not likely. I'll stick to raising the kids, thank you."

"Speaking of which, I think they need some attention right now," he commented dryly, directing her glance to the play-yard. Heidi had climbed high up in a tree and was ordering Jed to follow. Jed, apparently afraid to climb, yet afraid to disobey his big sister, stood at the bottom, protesting loudly.

"Heidi, come down from there this instant!" Cathy yelled.

"Can't," she answered in a matter-of-fact tone.

"Why not?"

"Cause Jed's not up here yet. He's 'sposed to come and rescue me."

"Some rescuer," Cathy said under her breath.

Robyn grinned. "That's what I would call a real knight in shining armor. He's more afraid than she is."

"Isn't that usually the case?"

"But don't forget who generally causes the problem in the first place," he countered. Nodding upward toward Heidi's precarious perch, he continued, "It's usually the female of the species who gets herself caught up in the tree!"

"Touché! But now how about some big strong male getting her down?"

Robyn bowed low. "No sooner said than done, m'lady."

He quickly scampered up the tree and brought Heidi down. "My charge for rescue service is one supper, served with a smile," he declared.

Cathy felt her pulses quicken involuntarily at his teasing. "But what about your guests?"

"No problem. They won't eat 'spirit food' anyway."

"Spirit food?"

"Anyone from another world is a spirit. These people only know one world, the forest that surrounds them. They can conceive of but one other place—the land of the dead. Consequently," he continued, "all of us foreigners came from the land of the dead."

Cathy shivered. "Spooky!"

"But perfectly logical to their limited experience. Obviously we lived here at one time and have come back to find out about our past lives—to relearn in our own village what we forgot on the long journey to that other world."

Hours later, Cathy tossed restlessly in her bed, unable to get thoughts of Robyn out of her mind. She must stop spending so much time with him. It could lead to nothing but heartbreak, and heaven knew she had had enough of that for one lifetime! Every time she closed her eyes, his blue eyes were smiling at her, his throaty voice echoing in her memory. *If this is a crush, I don't need it!*

Angrily, she threw back the mosquito netting and stalked over to the sink. She had never in her life let dishes sit until morning, and tonight was no time to start. She slammed the dishpan into the tiny sink and heated water on the Primus stove.

He has to be leaving before too long, she consoled herself. *And Bonnie and Joel will be back in a week or so. Surely, he can't do too much damage to my psyche in that short a time*. Or could he? Torn by doubt and dismay, she strolled out to the porch. A sliver of moon hovered over the forest, dappling the trees with ghostly shadows.

The myriad of daylight birds and insects had long ago returned to their resting places, and the creatures of the night began to stir and call.

Something deep within Cathy also began stirring—a yearning she had never before acknowledged, desires she hadn't known she was capable of.

She felt her resolve sinking, her armor splintering into a thousand pieces. No! She must stop this wayward course of her emotions, must get herself under control. She had to!

If only she had had a mother to teach her things, to

understand, to talk to! Unconsciously, she gave a characteristic defensive shrug. *Well, I didn't have, and there's no use crying over that!*

Whirling to go back into the house, she caught the heel of her slipper in the hem of her gown and stumbled forward. A strong arm suddenly reached out from the darkness, catching her. She felt the hard muscles pulling her toward the steadying length of his body, and the contact momentarily stilled her.

The unfamiliar touch of a man's hand seemed to burn through the thin fabric of her gown, and she reacted violently. "Let me go!" she screamed. "Let me go!"

"Shh," Robyn cautioned. "Do you want to wake the entire neighborhood?"

Cathy pulled away from him in the darkness. "What were you doing here anyway? Spying on me?"

Undaunted, Robyn offered, "I saw your light on and figured I might be able to entice you to go for a moonlight stroll. I couldn't sleep either."

"I wasn't having difficulty sleeping," she lied. "There's nothing around here that could keep me awake!"

Robyn grinned knowingly at her. "But psychiatrists prescribe moonlight strolls for pent-up frustration—"

"I am not frustrated!" she raged. "Now will you please let me get some sleep?"

He stepped aside. "Of course. But first, tell me, do you have to hate all men because you happened to have a bad experience with one of us?" The question was asked gently, searchingly.

His question stopped her, but she refused to turn around and look at him. "Good night, Mr. Harroway," she said as she started toward the door.

Unaware that the light streaming from the back door briefly silhouetted her feminine shape inside the silky peach-colored gown, she started at the sudden huskiness in Robyn's voice as he called, "Good night, Princess."

Princess, indeed! Tarnished harlot was a more apt description. She slammed the screen door, hard.

Cathy deliberately stayed in bed the next morning until she heard Robyn's Jeep leave the camp. Huge, dark circles under her eyes indicated how little she had slept. Restlessly, she got the children fed, dressed, and out to the play-yard, the tiny house cleaned, and the laundry on the line. There must be something else she could do, anything to quell this uneasiness in her spirit.

Glancing out the kitchen window, she was disconcerted to see Bate's huge brown eyes staring back at her. Indignantly, she rushed to the porch to run the older woman off, but compassion set in before she did. Obviously, Bate was simply curious about her strange way of life.

Approaching the native woman, Cathy timidly began, "*Apinun, Missus.*"

Bate grinned broadly, revealing empty holes where teeth had been. "*Apinun.*"

Having exhausted her entire supply of pidgin, Cathy smiled helplessly. How did one talk to someone without knowing the language?

Seeming to sense her dilemma, Bate motioned in the direction of Foroba, who was busily carving a bamboo stake. "*Bik man, bik man,*" she declared proudly.

Cathy smiled and nodded. Obviously, Foroba was a big man.

Bate then pointed toward Robyn's house, then to Cathy. "*Bik man? Bik man?*" This time there was an unmistakable question in her voice.

Cathy shook her head. How could she convey to this native that Robyn was not her man? Oh well, she reasoned, what difference did it make? Attempting to change the subject, she motioned toward the open door, in a gesture she hoped the native would understand was an invitation.

Again, Bate smiled broadly. Following Cathy into the house, she gleefully ran from one piece of furniture to another, stopping to admire the lamps, pillows, and strange books and pictures. "*Kago, kago,*" she exclaimed happily, running her fingers over the softness of Cathy's bedspread, fingering the wicker chairs, examining each item in minute detail.

"*Kago?*" Cathy searched her memory. What did "*kago*" mean? Impulsively, she reached into her jewelry box and handed a small, inexpensive ring to Bate. Reaching for Bate's hand to show her how to wear it, Cathy drew back in shock. All the fingers were gone from her left hand, with nothing but ugly, short stumps protruding from her otherwise healthy palm. Bate pulled her hand from Cathy's view, holding it behind her back. A tear welled up in her eyes, as she said softly, "*Chilrun. Bik man's chilrun.*"

Cathy's heart lurched at Bate's apparent sorrow. But what was she trying to tell her? What was the story behind the loss of her fingers? She made a mental note to ask Robyn when he came home, forgetting her resolve to avoid him at any cost.

Bate suddenly launched into what seemed to Cathy a myriad of questions, all in staccato pidgin. Cathy tried desperately to catch at least a word here and there. Whatever Bate was asking, it was apparent she was becoming very agitated because Cathy was not answering her questions.

Cathy spread her hands helplessly, signifying she did not understand. Slowly comprehending the problem, Bate put her hand to her own ear, as if to say, "I want to hear you."

Speaking slowly and softly, Cathy began talking about whatever came to mind, awkwardly describing the weather, the children, her hometown in the States. It was Bate's turn to listen intently, but her agitation didn't lessen. Instead, she grew increasingly frustrated and finally stalked out of the cottage in an angry rage.

"Well," Cathy murmured to herself. "So much for the good neighbor policy. I blew that one royally!" She called Heidi and Jed in for lunch, then put Jed down for his nap. She spent the afternoon playing with Heidi, carefully avoiding going outside for another encounter with her new neighbors.

She felt her pulses quicken as Robyn's Jeep entered the compound. Now that he was home, everything would be all right again, and she could relax.

His voice filled the tiny cottage. "Anybody home? How about a picnic tonight?"

Cathy jumped to her feet. "A picnic? How would we manage that?"

He grinned. "Simple. Look at this!" Producing a bag of sandwiches, chips, and pickles, he teased, "Doesn't that look like picnic fare?"

"But how...?"

"Had a visitor at the mine today who thought we might like some normal chow for a change. So he brought all kinds of goodies down to us from the gedunk at the main mining cafeteria. You've been feeding me all week, so I thought it only fair to share my largess with you!"

They packed the necessary utensils into the bag and followed the stream up to Rainbow Falls. It was a long walk, and Cathy was grateful for Robyn's help with the little ones.

The path finally broke out of the dense forest, and for a time they followed along the stream bank, enjoying the music of the splashing waters. Looking down into the forever rushing water, Cathy felt her chest tighten with the old familiar feeling of helplessness ...of being merely a twig bobbing out of control at the mercy of the onrushing stream.

Robyn caught her hand, as if to steady her step. "Beautiful, isn't it?" His gaze took in her loosely flowing hair, her slightly flushed face. "And you're beautiful, too," he murmured.

She quickly pulled her hand away from his and stuck it in her jeans pocket. She wasn't accustomed to being complimented, and didn't quite know how to handle it. How she wished she could be light and funny like Bonnie, knowing just what to say and how to say it! Realizing Robyn was still waiting for her to reply, she muttered numbly, "You don't have to keep reminding me!"

He pulled back and looked at her with an odd, searching gaze. "Sorry," he said simply and walked over toward the falls.

Dismally, she followed his steps. *Leave it to me to say something dumb*, she scolded herself. *Why am I such a perfect idiot?*

Heidi and Jed were already splashing happily in the small pool formed at the side of the waterfall. Cathy stopped and drew in her breath at the beauty of the falls—the rushing torrent breaking out of the deep green of the rain forest, hurling itself headlong out of the hills and over the boulders.

She pulled off her shoes, rolled up her jeans, and waded out to a large rock near where the children were playing. She watched silently as the water tumbled all around her, splashing wildly around the rocks, bubbles of foam spiraling and riding the crest to the outer banks. In the deep pools hollowed out by eons of time, she could see the dark shapes of fish darting around.

She glanced up in surprise as Robyn plopped down on the rock beside her. The burbling and chuckling of the river had drowned out his approach.

"Penny for your thoughts," he offered.

She dangled her feet aimlessly in the cold water. "Just watching the water rushing along. It seems to be eager to get somewhere, but how does it know where it's going?"

69

He leaned back against the boulder and studied her momentarily. "I think you're comparing the river to life, aren't you?"

She nodded, thankful that he seemed to understand her mood. For some reason, she was beginning to feel safe in his presence, knowing he wouldn't laugh at her thoughts or make fun of her awkwardness. "It just seems to follow along in the path someone has laid out for it, never knowing what's just around the bend, but rushing along eagerly anyway."

"The river does follow the path Someone has laid out for it," he said thoughtfully. "But so does life. That Someone is God, Cathy. He has laid out a perfect plan for each of our lives. And if we follow that path, we don't need to worry about what's around the bend."

She laughed, a hard, brittle sound. "Well, if God laid out the path of my life, he sure didn't chart a very good course!" She jumped down from the boulder, wading quickly back toward the shore. "I'm starved! Let's eat!"

Dusk fell swiftly, the forest shadows deepened, and the air began to cool before they finally picked up their picnic things and headed back down the path toward home.

Cathy and Robyn each carried a tired toddler on their backs as they hurried down the path, walking closely together in the light of Robyn's flashlight.

A loud crashing sound on the path in front of them startled Cathy, and she involuntarily fell against Robyn for protection. The warmth of his body against hers brought heat rushing to her flushed skin. Thankful for the darkness that hid her blushing cheeks, she gasped, "What was that?"

He flashed the light on up the trail, spotlighting the frightened features of their new neighbor. *"Jus' Foroba, Masta!"*

A quick consultation with Foroba revealed that his pigs had failed to come home with the setting sun. In panic, he was searching through the darkened forest for his lost wealth, his only claim to manhood.

"We'll put the children to bed, have Bate stay with them, and we'll come back and help him find his pigs," Robyn volunteered.

Cathy protested. "Leave the children with that woman? No way!"

"They will be perfectly safe. Bate is a real jewel when it comes to kids. She loves 'em. And we need you with us out here—you probably know this area better than either of us."

Cathy had to agree with the wisdom of that statement. She had spent many hours wandering through what she considered "her" forest, her special spot on earth. She had no fear of the dark, dense jungle, where solitude surrounded her, with no one but the animals and insects for company. It was people she had to be wary of!

They hastily put Heidi and Jed into their mosquito nettings, and Robyn gave Bate clear explanations in pidgin. Cathy marveled at his ease with the language, feeling a slight twinge of jealousy because she couldn't converse with the older woman.

Grabbing a couple of spare flashlights, they went back along the trail to find Foroba. He was crashing so wildly through the trees, yelling for his pigs, he wasn't difficult to locate.

"He'll wake the dead with all that yelling!" Robyn commented.

Together, they devised a search plan, with Cathy giving area descriptions to Robyn, who diligently passed them along to Foroba in his own tongue.

As they slashed their way through the jungle, Cathy inhaled deeply. She enjoyed the pungent odor of mossy jungle growth mingled with the scent of hibiscus, eucalyptus, and a myriad of flowers. Moonlight filtered through lofty treetops, leaving ghostly shadows and eerie shapes. She generally enjoyed her nocturnal walks in the forest, but tonight her emotions were going haywire. Robyn's nearness disturbed her senses and it was exceedingly difficult to keep her mind on the task at hand, finding those pigs.

They circled for what seemed to be hours, rendezvousing with Foroba at appointed check points. But they found no sign of the runaway pigs. Foroba began to get agitated, insisting his enemies had come to steal the pigs. Robyn assured him that was impossible, that no one could possibly know where he was hiding, that it was too far away from the village for anyone on foot to find them.

They decided the pigs definitely were not in the radius they at first had searched, so Cathy led them farther upstream, heading for an area with which she, too, was unfamiliar. As they climbed higher onto the ridges, they could hear the water coursing down the mountainside in a spider's web of streams and torrents. The roaring of many waters all but prohibited conversation as they trekked onward.

Finally, Robyn called a halt to their climb. "There's no way those pigs could have come this far," he declared. "Let's turn around and head back. We've apparently missed them somewhere along the way."

They turned in the darkness to retrace their steps. Coming to a fork in the stream, Cathy felt a momentary panic. Which was the stream they had followed? Not wanting the men to know she was uncertain, she headed for the left. "This way," she ordered, with an air of assurance she didn't feel.

The stream widened into an ever-shifting pattern of channels and mudbanks, stopping suddenly in a crescent-shaped lake, a chocolate-colored mess of backwater trapped by silt. "Something's wrong here," Robyn observed. "We didn't pass this oxbow on our way up."

"I think we're lost," Cathy admitted wearily. "We must have taken a wrong turn back there someplace."

Philosophical as always, Robyn simply shrugged.

"Well, let's just stay here and get some rest. We can find our way out in the morning."

"But the children!"

"They'll be fine. I told you Bate is completely reliable. Right now, I'm more worried about you. You look completely done in."

Cathy had to nod agreement to that. She couldn't remember ever having been so tired in her life. Thankful for the mosquito repellant they had sprayed on liberally before they started into the forest, she leaned back against a boulder on the lakeshore and fell into an exhausted sleep.

Chapter Seven

Cathy awoke with the strange sensation that the ground was shifting beneath her. Leaves rustled as if in a high wind, and as she adjusted her eyes to the pre-dawn grayness, she saw an incredible sight. Across the oxbow lake on the ridge, a long line of trees swayed in perfect rhythm, as though dancing in a chorus line.

She tried to rise to her feet, but the uncanny feeling of undulating earth made her reel about like a drunk person.

Robyn, awakened by the commotion, looked over at her and laughed. "Just a small earth tremor."

"I know, but that doesn't make it any easier to stand up!" She had experienced the frequent, slight earth tremors back at the house, but somehow, out here in the wild, they seemed a little more frightening.

"This is the most geologically unstable zone in the world," Robyn explained, as though talking to a tour-ist. "So we get plenty of earth tremors. None of them bad ones, fortunately."

"You forget, I've lived here for six months," Cathy reminded him. "I'm used to the tremors."

He grinned, a boyish smile that made her heart do flipflops. "But I notice you haven't learned how to walk during a tremor yet! Here, let me steady you."

He reached an arm around her waist, holding her

tightly. But instead of steadying her, his forceful hold on her body sent her into a tailspin. The trees swayed crazily above her head; the very earth seemed to spin dizzily. She pulled away. "I think I'll just sit down till it's over," she declared.

Robyn turned to Foroba, trying to get the man's mind off his troubles. Cathy could only catch an occasional phrase of their discussion, but noting her interest, Robyn began to translate for her.

"He's telling me how he came to be accused of sorcery. If anyone gets very sick, his clan immediately gather to discover who caused the illness. The men rehash the patient's life and involvements, and suspicion runs rampant. Who was he last seen with? Has anyone sold him anything lately? Does anyone have a score to settle with the sick man?"

"Such superstition!" Cathy interjected. "How can anyone believe illness is caused by another person?"

"Out here, it's easy to believe," he told her. "Witchcraft rules these woods. The sinister implication is that if you had close contact with the patient, you might have stolen a piece of hair, a nail clipping—some essence of your intended victim—and inserted it into a rotting banana tree. That would make your victim sick, and unless they catch you the patient will die."

"And what happens if he does die?"

"The clan elders gather in a secret clearing with wild opossums, believing the dead man's spirit takes refuge among the animals, waiting to name his enemy. They offer a sweet potato to a caged opossum, while the suspect's name is whispered. If the animal takes a bite, it indicates potential guilt, and the clan goes after the supposed killer."

"And what do they do if they catch him?" she asked breathlessly.

"He's only a suspect until proven guilty. The opossums are killed, and live caterpillars are wrapped in leaves, attached to the opossum limbs, and cooked.

Then the dead man's relatives examine the caterpillars for signs of life—conclusive proof of guilt. If the caterpillars are all dead, the trial is left hanging, and eventually they eat the opossums."

Cathy shuddered. "I think I'll settle for trial by jury!"

He laughed, a deep, throaty sound that warmed Cathy's heart. "Civilization does have a lot to offer!"

Glancing to the horizon where the sun was beginning to glow pink across the sky, he rose to his feet. "The earth has settled down, so we'd better get back to our pig hunt."

The going was much easier in the bright sunlight, and they were able to find their original trail without too much difficulty. By noon they had discovered the pigs' trail and herded the contrary porkers home, squealing and protesting.

"Aunt Cathy! Aunt Cathy!" Heidi yelled with delight as they approached the camp. "Bate is nice! Me and Jed like her lots!"

Relieved that the children were obviously well cared for, Cathy wondered how they had managed to converse with Bate. She smiled her thanks at the grinning woman and took Heidi and Jed into the house to prepare their lunch.

"She don't like you much," Heidi observed.

Cathy held her sandwich halfway between her plate and her mouth, shocked. "Who doesn't like me?"

"Bate."

"And how do you know that?"

"She told me. She thinks you're from the spirit world, and she's mad cause you won't tell her news about her dead children."

"And did you tell her I'm not a spirit?"

Heidi munched into her peanut butter and jelly sandwich, giving her a superior look. "Course not. She can't understand me."

Cathy pondered that bit of information in silence.

How could Heidi figure out what she herself could not understand?

Robyn poked his head in the door. "Can you spare a sandwich for a poor, starving pighunter?"

Cathy laughed. "If the poor, starving pighunter will settle for peanut butter and jelly, I can."

He pulled a chair out and joined them at the table. "This starving man would settle for anything right now!" As Cathy poured his tea, he commented seriously, "I understand you're having problems with your new neighbor."

She looked at him in surprise. "Bate told you, too?"

"What do you mean, 'too'? Who else did she tell?"

Cathy nodded toward Heidi. "She bent Heidi's ear about my lack of communication with the dead."

"It seems Bate wants news of her dead children from the spirit world. She figures we're from that other world and should be able to see and speak to her sons. She wants us to bring messages, and instead we only chatter about things of little importance. Can you blame her for being angry?"

"But what are we going to do about it?"

Robyn looked at her, a long, thoughtful look. "I don't know what you can do about it, but I'm trying to teach her about Jesus Christ, to set her free from her superstitions and witchcraft."

"Thanks a lot," she muttered. "That's what I would call a big help!"

"Actually, I think I've got Bate convinced that you know nothing about her sons, that you're not being deliberately mean in keeping information from her. Meanwhile, you can probably earn her confidence with a little *kago*."

"Kago?"

"Pidgin for 'cargo'—everything we whites have that didn't come from the forest. Your wristwatch, flashlights, household goods, and canned food. The natives think our manufactured goods are gifts from the spirit world, just as their own items from the forests were left here as gifts from their ancestors."

Cathy shook her head wonderingly. "No wonder Bate was so fascinated by my things."

"In her view of things, you obviously traffic with the dead, to have so many gifts from the spirit world. So, as you share little *kago* trinkets with her, she thinks a dead relative is giving them specifically to her. It makes for meaningful communication!"

Bolstered with her new knowledge of local culture, Cathy decided to try once again to earn Bate's friendship. "But only if you're here to interpret," she insisted to Robyn.

Together, they invited the curious couple into the house, where Cathy watched with delight as they admired her *kago*. From her jewelry box, she pulled a seldom-worn cross pendant and hung it around Bate's neck. Bate squealed with pleasure, running her good hand around its smooth surface lovingly. "*Chilrun, chilrun,*" she repeated softly. A beatific smile spread across her face, and her countenance radiated with love.

"She thinks it's a gift from her dead children," Robyn whispered.

The *bik man*, Foroba, harumphed noisily, not wanting to be identified with the weak emotions of silly women. He stalked importantly from the house, without a glance to his right or left.

"He'll be back shortly," Robyn prophesied. "Wait and see."

Sure enough, in a few moments, Foroba strolled back into the room, magnificently decorated with a two-foot-long bird of paradise plume protruding from his pierced nose.

Half frightened, Cathy whispered, "What does that mean?"

"Oh, he's just strutting his stuff. That plume is to make him look his most manly, to make certain we don't identify him too closely with Bate."

"Why, that's silly! What's wrong with showing a little emotion?"

Robyn shrugged, the corners of his eyes crinkling in little wrinkles Cathy had come to expect when he was teasing. "Surely you've already discovered this is a land of male dominance. We men must blatantly look down upon you females as inferiors. We wouldn't dare admit female creativity is the ultimate source of power and progeny!"

"I don't think that kind of thinking is native to this land," she commented ruefully.

"Aha, I see I still haven't convinced you that we males are good company. Give me time, I'll win you over yet."

He nodded toward Foroba, who was just as interested in all Cathy's *kago* as was his wife, but who was carefully concealing his interest and keeping a safe distance from Bate. "That bird of paradise plume has special meaning to the men here. They teach their boys that all birds are created female, but some decorate themselves with bright feathers in order to become gorgeous males. So when a boy becomes a man, he puts on plumage to broadcast the fact that he is a male, symbolically reborn, and free from female domination."

"Sounds like they have a real battle of the sexes here," she commented.

"That's putting it mildly. Men hold their women in open contempt, considering them mentally inferior and dangerously contaminating." His expression softened, taking on an almost sensuous look. "I'm beginning to see the wisdom of their thinking. I could become contaminated by a certain woman very quickly."

Although she knew he was joking, his words stung. With her past, she would truly contaminate any man. Somehow, she would have to halt this growing friend-

79

ship with Robyn before it got out of hand. She wasn't worthy of his friendship and, most certainly, not of his love.

"I think I'd like to rest now," she declared, a note of irritation in her voice. "Can you get your friends out of my house for a while?"

He quirked an eyebrow at her sudden mood swing, but acquiesced without comment. He soon convinced Foroba and Bate it was time to leave, and Cathy gladly ushered them all to the door.

She really was tired. Last night's long trek through the woods hadn't afforded much rest. Her leg muscles ached with a constant throb, and her head was pounding violently. She didn't often succumb to tension headaches, but then, until Robyn's arrival, she hadn't had much tension.

She took an aspirin, coaxed Jed to sleep, and sent Heidi out to follow Robyn around. After all, she reasoned, her headache was his fault, so he could look after Heidi for her. Even as she sent the little girl outside, however, she felt a sharp twinge of conscience. She had never shifted her responsibilities onto anyone else, had never wanted to.

Stranger yet was her willingness to trust Robyn with Heidi. A few weeks ago, she would never have entrusted her darling niece to any man's company. Men were too devilish, too untrustworthy. What was there about Robyn that incited so much trust? She yawned and crawled thankfully onto the cot. A good nap would help her get her thoughts in order and think through the situation.

A loud ruckus in the play-yard aroused her. She dashed outside in time to hear Jed yowling heartily and Bate and Foroba arguing. Robyn came running from the other side of the camp.

"What's going on?" she asked indignantly. "How did Jed get out here?"

Robyn glanced at his watch. "You've been asleep for four hours. When Jed woke up, I brought him out and asked Bate to watch him."

"Four hours!" Cathy was instantly ashamed. She never took naps and certainly not when the children were in her care. What if one of them got hurt?

As if reading her thoughts, Robyn calmed her fears. "It's all right. You needed to sleep; you were nearly exhausted. The kids were fine here with Bate until Foroba decided to exercise his manly rights."

"Manly rights?" Instantly, Cathy ran to Heidi. "Did he hurt you?"

Heidi looked at her in disgust. "Won't even pay any 'tention to me. He says he has to make Jed act like a man. He got mad because Jed was crying and acting like a sissy. And when Bate hugged Jed, he *really* got mad!"

Robyn finished the explanation. "You've just witnessed the local version of antagonism between the sexes. Bate was exercising her maternal rights in raising the male child, and Foroba insisted on his prerogative to transform Jed into a man." He shrugged indifferently. "It's a daily occurrence in a Bsorio village. You get used to the ways of men after a while."

She knew he was mocking her, knew that he sensed the upheaval he was causing in her very soul. Somehow, she had to bring him down a peg. "Sir," she began, bowing low. "Your extreme fascination is only superseded by your deep humility!" Whirling on her heels, she stomped toward the house. She slammed the door, but not in time to shut out the sound of his deep chuckle.

As Cathy spent more time with Bate and Foroba, she found her understanding of the pidgin language increasing with surprising swiftness. More surprising was the ease with which Heidi and Jed picked up the language. Discussing the situation with Robyn one evening, she said, "I still can't understand how these kids pick it up so quickly. It's almost as though they're conversing in their own language."

"Basically, it is their own tongue," he observed. "Pidgin is a form of English, broken down to its simplest phonetic syllables. And isn't that how babies speak? Listen to Jed rattling off over there...'*drinka wara*'...you know he wants a drink of water, don't you?"

Cathy laughed. "You're right! He's been speaking pidgin all along! No wonder Heidi understands Bate and Foroba so well—she often has to interpret Jed's pidginese for me!"

She grew serious. "But it was a bit difficult today when Bate wanted some information on how to get her *bik man* to love her better. Try discussing love and affection through a five-year-old interpreter!"

He tilted his chair back, gazing at her with eyes full of tenderness. "Even native women need affection from their menfolk, don't they?"

She sipped her lemonade, afraid of where this conversation was leading, afraid of that lustrous gleam in his eyes. Finally, she spoke. "It's just that Foroba treats her with such disdain, like she's a nonperson. Yet, when he thinks no one is watching, it looks like he absolutely yearns with love for her."

Taking in her dubious expression, he shrugged. "Simply the way of the native New Guinean. Their male rituals enact myths that exalt women's creative powers. It's a standing sore point to the males that they cannot give birth to progeny, so all their lives are spent denying maternal influence and asserting the importance of being masculine. Secretly, they envy the women and want to please them."

"They sure have some crazy ideas. Almost as bad as American men."

The crinkles appeared around his eyes again. "And by implication, I'm sure you are also referring to us Aussies?"

"If the shoe fits, wear it!"

Cathy wanted to laugh, to relax and enjoy this light-hearted sparring, but part of her held back. She would probably say something dumb or perhaps learn to enjoy his company too much and end up getting hurt again. "Tell me more about their rituals," she said, finally breaking the uncomfortable silence she had brought about.

"Flutes are prime symbols of all fertility here," he explained. "And they once belonged only to the women, until some brave warriors stole them. Now that the men possess the flutes, they too have the power to give birth."

She quirked an eyebrow. "Men have power to give birth? How so?"

"It's part of their initiation ordeal. When boys reach their young adolescent years, they are taken in to the men's houses and kept sleepless and thirsty for days. Figures shrouded in rustling leaves and hideous mud-caked masks snake through the houses, hissing, lunging at the boys with stone axes."

He cleared his throat. "The threatened carnage is stopped short when a number of men playing flutes emerge suddenly from the jungle. This is a tremendous revelation to the boys, who have heard the wondrous flute sounds all their lives and have been taught they come from fabulous birds, hidden from women but associated with men."

Cathy's eyes widened with interest. "How do you know all this?"

"I went to one of their initiation rituals with Pete Ellis," he answered. "Anyway, as the flute sounds fade, the instructor tells them the flutes once belonged to the women, but the men took them away forever, by trickery. The dazed boys are threatened with death if they ever tell any of this to a female!"

"Finally," he continued, "on the last day of the ceremonies, the boys emerge at noon, borne on the shoulders of soot-blackened warriors, each boy gleaming red from head to toe, covered with pandanus nut oil."

Cathy shuddered. "Ugh!"

"It is rather a repulsive sight, but designed to simulate the blood of birth. Bright red parrot feathers and golden plumes from birds of paradise adorn the boys, signifying they are at long last separated from their mothers and have been reborn as independent men. From that moment on, no self-respecting *bik man* will bow to female dominance."

"But showing a little affection isn't bowing to any dominance!" Cathy protested.

"Ah, but it is," he argued, leaning over close to her. "You women with your feminine wiles have but to crook your finger, and we poor males come running. So, in order to stay free, we have to keep a safe distance!"

She knew he was teasing, but nevertheless, her pulses began racing madly. Never would she crook her finger to any man. She didn't want to dominate anyone. She just wanted the male of the species to leave her alone!

She watched Robyn walk across the room and speak to Jed. "Come on, fella, time for bed!" Putting his hand lightly on Jed's shoulder, he steered him toward the lavatory for his evening washup. The little boy followed him eagerly, his eyes shining with trust and admiration. What was it that Mr. Jordan always used to say? Something about "You can always trust a man who loves children and dogs"?

If that truly was a guideline for trust, Robyn surely deserved it. She was awed by his complete ease with Heidi and Jed, his compassion and friendship with Bate and Foroba. It seemed he always knew just when and how to encourage, to comfort, or to set things straight when needed. A woman ought to be able to trust a man like that, she thought wonderingly.

She had to quit thinking like this. No man could be

trusted! Impatiently she headed for Heidi. "Come on, Heidi, let's get you ready for bed."

When both children were safely tucked in bed, Robyn headed for the door. "Take a walk with me in the moonlight?" he invited casually.

The look of eager anticipation in his eyes made her breathless, yet frightened. She stammered hurriedly, "Uh, I don't think so...not tonight."

For a moment he hesitated, unsure if he should press the invitation. Then he took another step toward her, his arm reaching out. "Just for a while. I feel like talking."

Again she evaded him, a look of uneasiness clouding her eyes. She put up a shaking hand to stop him. "No!"

For a moment they stood a few paces away from each other, their eyes clinging. Robyn drew a long, deep breath and said very gently, "I'll keep my distance, I promise."

Suddenly, he grinned at her, and a warm feeling flooded her soul. It was as though something deep within her heart had listened and responded to something in his. In a tremulous voice, she said, "Let's go. But only for a short walk."

They walked silently out into the star-studded night. Cathy breathed deeply of the heavily scented tropical air, feeling the slight breeze kiss her hot skin and lift her hair ever so slightly.

"Those palm trees look like giant feather dusters stretching up to clean the sky," Robyn observed aloud.

She stared at him in amazement. "Why, that's exactly what I was thinking! Did you read my thoughts?"

"I wish I could," he teased. "Then I wouldn't have to waste so much time trying to second guess you."

She was instantly alert. "Why bother?"

He stopped short, turning to face her. "You don't have a very high opinion of yourself, do you?"

She looked at him through downswept lashes. "I get

along with myself fairly well. It's other people who disturb me."

"We're going to have to work on that," he murmured softly.

She was instantly on guard, her fists clenching at her side. "I don't need any help. I was perfectly satisfied with my life until you came along." Too late, she realized her admission. Thankful for the darkness which hid her flaming face, she muttered, "It doesn't matter anyway."

Robyn spoke with quiet emphasis. "It matters to me. It matters a whole lot." His eyes studied her in the semi-darkness. Suntanned, regal, her dark hair ruffled by the breeze that had tugged its binding ribbon loose, she seemed oblivious to the beguiling picture she made. He reached out and removed the loose ribbon, letting her hair tumble like a curtain over her shoulders. "You are simply beautiful!" he remarked softly.

She pulled away in alarm, so startled she couldn't speak.

Without warning, his arms swept around her, and he held her close, moving his rough, large hands gently up and down her back. He continued to stroke her hair, sending tremors vibrating through her.

She gasped for breath, enjoying the feel of his hands touching her hair and shoulders.

With supreme effort, she pulled desperately away. Retying her hair ribbon, as if somehow the activity would cleanse her emotions, she turned swiftly back toward the house.

With uncharacteristic anger, Robyn demanded, "You're treating me like a walking contagious disease! I'm only trying to help!"

Cathy caught her breath on a gasp of sheer outrage. "I don't need that kind of help."

Anger still riding high in his eyes, he countered, "You mean you don't *want* my kind of help. It's abundantly clear that you need help!"

"When I want anybody's help, I'll ask for it. Until then, I'll thank you to keep your opinions of my psychological hangups to yourself." Turning abruptly from him once more, she stumbled over a large root in the path and sprawled ignominiously to the ground.

Robyn looked down at her, the faintest hint of a grin touching the corners of his mouth. "I would be a gentleman and offer to help you up, but I don't dare. A certain little spitfire told me I couldn't offer my help until she asked for it."

"You...you...rotten *man*!" she exploded. Breathless and outraged, she threatened, "I'd lie here and die before I asked for your help!"

He apologized with unexpected humility, tucking the words in neatly while he reached down strong, muscled arms to lift her to her feet. "I'm sorry. But you do matter to me, and I intend to help you whether you want it or not."

On the point of flight, Cathy hesitated, wanting terribly to believe him, to trust him, to have him as a friend. Unconscious of the fact he was still holding lightly onto her hand, she offered a truce. "I believe we were taking a walk?"

Side by side they strolled along the creek bank, staying on the edge of the forest. They passed several small inlets, and Robyn automatically tightened his clasp to help her over the slippery rocks.

He led the way, veering off the beaten track, his arm still lightly around her shoulder, as if to protect her. It was a disconcerting sensation, yet a welcome one, as if her safety really mattered to someone. They climbed slowly up the ridge, coming to a clearing, a small, grass-covered slope.

"Look down there," he suggested.

Below, coconut palms and a riot of jungle vegetation stood like sentinels. They clearly outlined the river as it broke out of the dense forest and tumbled in a froth of white foam over the steep cliff.

"Why, that's Rainbow Falls!" Cathy exclaimed. "How did we get above it?"

His voice strangely gentle, Robyn answered. "A trail I discovered the other evening. But I didn't know it was called Rainbow Falls."

There was the slightest of pauses before she replied. "That's just a name I gave it. It's a special place to me, especially when the early morning sun makes tiny rainbows in the mist coming up from the falls."

His arm tightened ever-so-imperceptibly around her shoulder. "Do you realize God has been sending rainbows for thousands of years for our enjoyment? I wonder how many lovers have stood in awe at the majesty of a rainbow, never thinking of God's promise that goes along with it."

Cathy didn't speak, but pulled slightly away from his hold. Lovers? Had he implied that they were lovers? Surely not. Surely he was just being kind to her, sympathetic even. A man with Robyn's compassionate nature would look on her as a lost kitten to be rescued. And men didn't fall in love with lost kittens!

Even as she pulled away, however, she felt his arm constrict, threatening to tighten should she try to escape. She sighed, a relaxed kind of sound.

"We'll have to come out here some morning, so I can see your rainbows," he suggested, as they headed back down the path. "Do you ever take an early morning swim?"

She hesitated. She loved her moments alone in the deep pool at the base of the falls, moments of privacy she usually snatched before the children were awake. The cool water splashing like a spring shower over her naked shoulders seemed to wash away the sorrows and disappointments momentarily. Somehow, she didn't want to share that privacy with anyone—not even Robyn, who was fast becoming the closest thing to a friend she had ever had.

Realizing she still hadn't answered his question, she

blurted, "Oh, no, the kids keep me much too busy for that."

"Maybe some morning Bate can stay with them while I bring you out to look for rainbows. But it will have to wait a few days. I'm going to be gone the next couple of days."

"Gone?" Her heart lurched. Being alone had never bothered her before, but now the thought of his leaving disturbed her, more than she cared to admit even to herself.

"They need me to check out some equipment at the main mine. Should only take a day or so, but it might stretch into a tougher job." He gave her a gentle, searching look. "You'll be all right here, won't you?"

She stood still, ignoring the chatter of the birds and the movement of the wind in the palms. Something in his eyes compelled her to bite back the flippant retort which had sprung to her lips. Suddenly it was very important that she say the right thing.

"I'll be fine." She hesitated, then added candidly, "but lonely."

The pause between them was electric. A slow, caressing smile curled the corners of Robyn's mouth. "I was hoping you'd say that."

Chapter Eight

Cathy spent the next few days learning local gardening techniques from her new friends. And they were her friends. She enjoyed talking with them, laughing with them at her clumsy pidgin. Bate's full, throaty laughter often erupted from her wide, toothless mouth and rang through the camp.

Cathy noticed a change in Foroba's demeanor, also. With no other men in the area and thus no danger of losing face, he gave Bate an affectionate touch now and then, a touch which always brought a light into Bate's sad eyes.

Bate's innate sadness remained an enigma to Cathy. She could only ascertain that it had something to do with Bate's dead children. It was a subject Bate refused to discuss.

Apparently, Robyn or the Ellises had told the native couple a good bit about the Christian religion, for they often asked Cathy questions about Jesus, questions she had difficulty answering. They often sat and listened to Heidi sing the Sunday school songs Robyn had taught her.

"Jesus loves the little children, all the children of the world. Short and fat and awful dumb, Jesus loves us everyone, Jesus loves the little children of the world!" she lisped.

"Heidi!" Cathy scolded. "That's not the way that song goes. Where did you ever hear that?"

"No place. I just made it up."

"Well, it's not very nice," Cathy admonished.

"'Tis too nice," Heidi defended. "Uncle Rob says Jesus loves all of us, and it don't matter what we look like or what we've done, or if we're dumb or smart!"

The sound of a machete striking wood interrupted Cathy's reply. She turned to see Foroba swinging at a huge smoke bush near Robyn's house. "Why are you cutting that down?" she asked.

He looked up momentarily from his work. "Roots under house."

She saw the roots were indeed spreading under the house, causing upheaval in the foundation. She stepped back as he continued to chop at the bush, making sure Jed and Heidi were safely out of harm's way from falling branches.

Unexpectedly, Bate jumped up in alarm. "No! No!" she protested, pointing to a small bird nest shaking precariously from the branches of the doomed tree.

But it was too late. The large bush, too far gone to rescue, plummeted to the ground with a loud crash! Miraculously, Foroba caught the bird nest in mid-fall, rescuing it and the three tiny blue eggs it contained.

Bate studied the eggs, her eyes filling with huge tears. She shook her head from side to side, all the time muttering, *"Chilrun, chilrun. Burd's chilrun."*

Cathy watched with dismay as the parent birds fluttered hopelessly about the area, looking for their home and their offspring. Impulsively, she took the nest from Bate's hand and waved it slowly through the air, hoping to coax the birds back to it.

Her motions only frightened the excited birds, however, so she carefully placed the nest on the smoke bush stump. Perhaps they would recognize it as home. All afternoon, the mother bird fluttered and cried, a mournful sound that only heightened Bate's melancholy.

That night, Cathy took the nest inside the house, feeling an urgent need to protect the eggs from the predators she knew lurked about. Somehow, she had to save those eggs! If only Robyn were here tonight, she reasoned, he would know what to do about the bird nest. If there were a way to save it, he would surely find it.

She slept lightly, her subconscious always tuned for the sound of his vehicle, but no approaching wheels roused her.

Waking before dawn, she dressed for an early swim under her oversize shirt. But once outside, she went to inspect the smoke bush stump. The mother and father bird were perched in a tree nearby, still keeping a watchful eye on the area. *Oh, if only I could talk to them*! Cathy thought.

In the dim predawn light, she hurried down the forest path, her steps light on the mossy trail. The heat was already rising without a hint of breeze to help her tolerate the oppressive humidity. Perspiration trickled down her spine and formed a tiny rivulet in the hollow between her breasts. Her shirt clung to her damp skin, and she tasted the salt of her own perspiration on her lips. The pool would be especially inviting this morning.

She reached Rainbow Falls just as the first rays of the sun were streaking the sky, and began to unbutton her sweat-damp shirt.

"Good morning, Princess!"

Cathy started at the familiar voice. "Robyn? What are you doing here?"

"Came to see your rainbow." He climbed up out of the pool, water dripping from faded cut-offs. "Got home in the middle of the night and couldn't sleep for the heat."

"But…but…I didn't hear your Jeep," she stammered.

"I shut off the engine and the lights and coasted in so I wouldn't wake anyone." Reaching for her arm, he coaxed, "Come on in. The water's fine."

Torn between her desire for the cool water and her discomfort at being seen without her protective shirt, she hesitated.

Sensing her reluctance, Robyn promised, "I'll look the other way until you're in the pool. It really does feel too good to miss."

As he turned from her, she peeled off her outer clothing. Self-conscious in her two-piece swimsuit, she quickly dived in, reveling in the refreshing feel of water on her hot, flushed skin.

"Fantastic, isn't it?" he began, swimming over to where she was standing almost neck-deep under the chilly spray. He reached out and flicked a small twig from her bare shoulder, a touch that sent her senses reeling.

"Did you miss me?" he asked, smiling.

She shivered. "Yes, I did. The kids and I had a great time getting to know Foroba and Bate, but the evenings were awfully long."

Her answer brought a strange, happy light to his eyes. "I missed you, too. I was getting used to those long, quiet talks we've enjoyed every evening after supper."

She stood utterly still before him in the water, her mind groping for words. How she wished for the ability to flirt, to bat her eyes coquettishly, to say something witty. Instead, she skimmed the top of the water with both hands out to the side and erupted with a long recitation of everything that had happened during his absence—Foroba's new deference to Bate, Heidi's silly new words to the songs he had taught her, even Bate's sadness at the dislodged bird nest.

Robin made little response, and they both swam a

few easy laps across the stream. As Cathy climbed out of the water, she was vibrantly aware of Robyn's appraisal of her long, lean limbs. Hastily, she grabbed her shirt from the bush on which she had hung it and tossed it around her still-wet swimsuit. The shirt was instantly damp and clung sensuously to her. As she started toward home, Robyn was at her side.

They walked in silence for a few minutes before Cathy lamented, "I've tried everything to show those birds where their nest is, but I can't get through to them. And poor Bate is half out of her mind with despair for them!"

He fingered her wet hair, brushing it away where it clung to her damp cheek. "That's why God had to come to earth, to become a human being," he mused.

Her eyebrows shot up in a delicate question. "What has God got to do with my bird nest?"

"The only way you could talk to those birds and explain where their nest is would be to become a bird, right?"

She nodded thoughtfully. "I suppose so...they sure don't understand anything else. I've even tried yelling at them in pidgin," she said ruefully.

He laughed. "That's exactly how it was with God. He wanted so desperately to communicate with us, to show us he cared for us, yet we couldn't understand him. So he came in the flesh, in the form of Jesus, to become one of us—someone who spoke our language, who could feel our hurts, share our sorrow, and tell us about heaven."

Cathy allowed this strange new thought into her consciousness. "I have to admit, it sounds logical," she said, plunging out into deeper water for one last refreshing dip. "But that still doesn't solve my problem with the birds!"

"Look, Aunt Cathy!" Heidi demanded as they approached the yard. "Foroba put the tree up!"

Somehow, he had managed to restore the smoke

bush to its stump, holding it in place with vines tied tightly to the house. Nestled securely in its branches was the nest, the mother bird chirping happily on her eggs. Her gay chirping was nothing compared to Bate's excited chatter. "*Bik man, bik man*," she exulted proudly. "*Bik man* fix anything."

From the corner of her eye, Cathy noted the glow on Foroba's face, the thinly disguised gleam of pride at his woman's praise.

The days that followed fell into a pattern, with Cathy tending the children all day, eagerly looking forward to Robyn's return each evening. Their evenings of sharing and talking together had become the highlight of her days.

Almost unconsciously, she wore the dark glasses less often, and even occasionally let her shiny tresses fall freely, but Robyn said nothing about the change in her appearance.

On the night before Bonnie and Joel's scheduled arrival home, Cathy and Robyn were sitting on the love seat in comfortable silence, the only sound the beating of rain upon the tin roof.

"This is almost as bad a storm as the one I blew in on," Robyn observed.

Cathy, feeling oddly restless, swung her legs to the floor and wandered over to the window. "I thought this was supposed to be the dry season."

"The dry season doesn't mean we don't get any rain," Robyn explained. "It just means we don't get as much. Actually, there are two seasons—wet and not quite so wet!"

Changing the subject abruptly, he asked, "What are your plans for Christmas?"

She spun around from the window. "Christmas?"

"Yes, Christmas. You know, the holiday when all is merry? It's only a few weeks away."

Cathy walked over to the calendar. "You're right!

These crazy seasons—with no frost in the air or snow on the ground, Christmas has sneaked right up on me."

The sound of Robyn's laughter filled the room. "Spoken like a true Pennsylvania mountain woman! Anyway, how would you like to spend Christmas down under?"

Cathy's enormous green eyes widened. "Down under? In Australia?"

He nodded. "I get two weeks holiday from the mine and thought I'd pay a respectful-son visit home. It would be a whole lot pleasanter if you were with me."

Cathy's voice held a tinge of wonder. "You want me to go with you?" Reality suddenly set in. "Oh, but I couldn't. Bonnie and Joel said something about spending the holidays in Port Moresby. I'm sure they expect me to take care of the kids."

"They would leave you here alone at Christmas?"

"Oh no. They would book a room for me, too."

"I'm sure they would. They'd go out and see the sights and do the town, secure in the knowledge that their faithful little nanny was on the job."

"But they need me," she protested, her voice tiny.

"Well, maybe I need you, too! When are you going to start living your own life instead of existing on the fringes of Bonnie's life?"

His words stung her to the depths, their truthfulness rubbing raw wounds. Her breath congealed in her lungs, and she felt she would suffocate. "You...you don't understand," she whispered.

"I'm trying to understand," he thundered. "But you can't let what happened to you warp the rest of your life!"

She gave a bitter laugh. "You don't know the first thing about it, so don't presume to offer advice."

Robyn sat back on the love seat, his head in his hands. "You're not the only person in this world who had a rotten childhood. My father wasn't the greatest, either. He abused me plenty."

Cathy shot him a questioning look, and Robyn shook his head. "No, not physically. But his dictatorial, demanding ways practically ruined me. For years I couldn't do anything right, and my self-image was rock-bottom."

Cathy sat down next to him again. "But you seem so confident and self-assured. What happened?"

He gazed directly into her eyes, a look that sent her pulses racing. "I met Jesus Christ, and He changed my life completely. I still feel twinges of bitterness now and then toward my father," he admitted. "But mostly, I've been able to forgive him."

"I could never forgive my foster father," Cathy blurted. "Never!"

He looked at her tenderly. "Not on your own, you couldn't. But Jesus Christ can fill you with a love that's unbelievable."

"Well, I'm glad it worked for you. But I don't want to forgive him, and I'm not hankering to join any religion."

Robyn sighed a sigh of resignation. "Anyway, would you reconsider and spend Christmas with me? It would be good for Heidi and Jed to spend some time with their parents, and I do need you."

She paced the room, her face full of uncertainty. "In what way do you need me?"

"For moral support. I still have difficulty standing up to Dad, and he's determined to get me married off to Sylvia."

"Sylvia?"

"The woman whose parents own the adjoining spread. Remember the happy merger Dad had in mind?"

Cathy nodded. "But how can my being there help?"

A sheepish look on his face, Robyn explained. "If I bring a gorgeous woman home with me, they'll figure I'm attached, and maybe Dad will lay off my back."

As the intent of his words soaked in, Cathy gasped. "But that's deceitful!"

"No, it's not," he argued. "We'll tell them we're good friends, which is true, and they can draw their own conclusions."

She remained doubtful. "I don't know. Anyway, I don't feel comfortable among strangers, and I don't have any clothes except jeans."

He had an answer for every objection. "It's just a small sheep station. You lived on a farm with the Jordans in Pennsylvania, didn't you?"

"Yes, but..."

"No but's about it. As for clothes, we can stop in Port Moresby and pick up a couple of outfits. Since you're doing this as a favor to me, the least I can do is provide the costumes."

"I still haven't said I'll go."

"But you will, won't you?" His voice took on a pleading tone she couldn't resist.

"We'll see. But you'll have to clear it with Bonnie and Joel—I can't say no to them any easier than I can to you," she sighed.

The pounding of the rain on the roof echoed the pounding of her heart that night, as she tossed restlessly. Australia! A sheep station! She hugged her pillow close, a contented smile playing across her face. Maybe, just maybe, life was brightening up a little.

Chapter Nine

Driving to meet Bonnie and Joel at their rendezvous point the next day, Cathy felt strangely reluctant to tell them about Robyn. Yet she knew she had to bring up the subject. How to do it? She needn't have worried. The minute they were all seated in the Land Rover, the greeting hugs and kisses finished, the loquacious Heidi talked non-stop about their new neighbor all the way home.

When Robyn joined them for supper, Bonnie flipped her long blonde braid over her shoulder and teased, "Cathy in the same room with a man! I just can't believe my eyes!"

"Tell me, Robyn," she continued. "How did you pull it off? Have you hypnotized her? Or maybe you've drugged her!"

Cathy squirmed uncomfortably, her face flaming. But Bonnie and Joel seemed oblivious to her discomfort. They prattled on about her fear of men, almost as though she weren't even in the room.

"Remember that time we fixed her up with Harry what's-his-name?" Joel joked.

"Yeah—she huddled in the corner of the car the entire evening, and as soon as we got home, she jumped out and ran into the house, leaving old Harry standing there with his mouth open!"

Bonnie burst into a fit of giggles, remembering. "I'll never forget the time the salesman came to the door and Cathy hid under the table!"

"Yes, sir, Robyn," Joel smirked. "Somehow you've managed to tame a real man-hater there."

Noticing Cathy's stricken face, Robyn answered coldly, "I think that's enough humor at Cathy's expense for one evening. How was your trip?"

Relieved at the change of subject, Cathy washed the dishes, listening absently as they discussed their linguistic work, surprised at how conversant Robyn was on the subject. *Probably picked it up from the missionaries*, she mused.

Her reverie was abruptly shattered when she heard her name enter the conversation again. "And so," Robyn was saying, "I've invited Cathy to spend the holidays with me in Australia."

The dish she was wiping clattered loudly to the floor as she heard Bonnie's shocked reply. "Now really, Rob, isn't that being a bit precipitous? I mean, we hardly know you. We can't let her go wandering off with the first man who happens along."

Cathy flung the dishtowel into the sink with disgust. "Good gosh, Bonnie," she cried. "You sound as if you're talking about a child! I'm twenty-five years old, fully capable of making my own decisions." She paused to catch her breath. Was she really talking back to the irrepressible Bonnie? She could hardly believe her own voice.

Bonnie, too, was noticeably surprised by her outburst, but quickly regained control of the situation. "Of course you're twenty-five. But a very naive twenty-five. We just don't want you to get hurt."

Hurt? What did Bonnie know about hurt? "It's only a holiday in Australia, for Pete's sake," she said tiredly. "And I'll only be gone two weeks or so. Surely you can manage Heidi and Jed for that long."

"Of course, we can manage. But we did want you to

enjoy Port Moresby with us. You've been stuck here so long."

Once again, Robyn came to Cathy's rescue. "We plan to see Port Moresby on our way through; then I hope to show Cathy the sights of Northern Australia."

"And it's a great opportunity to see a real sheep station in operation," Cathy cut in.

Joel grinned sardonically. "Sheep station? We might as well give up, Bonnie. You know we can't compete with Cathy's love affair with sheep."

Robyn shot her a quizzical glance. "Love affair with sheep?"

Cathy tried to pass it off. "Just a family joke."

"Our Cathy is far too modest," Joel continued. "Didn't she tell you she has a degree in animal husbandry with a major in sheep diseases?"

Robyn's normally bright blue eyes turned dark and foreboding. "No, she didn't tell me."

Bonnie rose from the wicker chair and yawned. "I'm exhausted. I'll just leave Heidi and Jed here tonight. They're sleeping so well, I hate to wake them."

Joel joined her at the door. "Besides, if they stay here, we can sleep in tomorrow, right?"

Bonnie laughed, a delightful little tinkle. "Right, darling!"

"Why do you let them walk all over you like that?" Robyn insisted, as soon as they had closed the door.

Cathy pushed a stray lock of hair back into place. "I told you—Bonnie's done a lot for me. I owe it to her."

Robyn shook his head in disgust. "A college degree in a field you obviously love, and you're stuck out here like a...like a common babysitter!"

"Maybe I like babysitting," she murmured.

"I have to admit you're good at it. But someone with your looks and talents should be caring for her own babies."

A grey pallor swept over Cathy's face, and she began to tremble. Robyn was immediately at her side.

"What's wrong? What did I say? What's so frightening about having your own little ones to care for?"

His machine-gun questions evoked no response from the ashen-faced Cathy, who sat biting her lip and fighting back tears.

"Please talk to me," he pleaded. "Don't shut me out like this."

Avoiding his gaze, she studied the pattern in the straw rug, kicking at it with the toe of her sneaker. From somewhere deep within her, she summoned the courage to meet his gaze. "You might as well know the whole sordid mess. Remember, I told you once about my first foster father, that he wanted me to be his 'good little girl'? He abused me, Robyn—sexually."

Robyn sat in silence. Then he said, "I guessed it might be something like that. No wonder you don't trust anybody. But it wasn't your fault—you can't take the blame for something you couldn't control. How old were you?"

"Fourteen."

His fists clenched into tight knots at his sides. "I'd like to strangle the jerk!" he exploded. "But what he did to you wasn't your fault."

Cathy shuddered at the horrible memories. "But it was my fault—Mom said if I wasn't so beautiful, Chester wouldn't have bothered me. I hate being beautiful!" she exclaimed bitterly.

Robyn's face was a strange mixture of rage and understanding. "That's why you're so afraid to let your beauty show...."

"I can't stand for men to look at me with that...like that...," she choked.

"But not all of us are like that. Sure, any man who isn't blind would admire you, but not with bad intentions. At least they'd better not try it while I'm around!" he teased gently. "Now, try to get some shut-eye. Maybe you can practice counting sheep to prepare for our trip."

Cathy looked up at him, her tear-brimmed eyes wide with incredulity. "You still want me to go with you?"

Robyn headed for the door. "Of course—why not?"

The days before their departure passed swiftly, and Cathy was relieved that there seemed to be no difference in Robyn's attitude toward her. What kind of man was he, to be so understanding, so kind and good?

On the morning they were to leave for the Goroka airfield, Robyn decided that he and Cathy would take Bate and Foroba back to their home in the Bsorio village. Foroba, all atwitter with obvious delight at the upcoming ride in Robyn's Jeep, loaded his pigs into the back, and they were off.

Miles rushed quickly by, with Cathy and Rob delighting in the enjoyment of their passengers. Depositing Bate and Foroba back at their old hut, they were greeted with a flurry of hellos and good-byes from the Ellises, amidst promises to come and visit when they returned. Finally, they were again on their way.

As they sped along the Highlands Highway toward Goroka, Cathy felt almost carefree. The road twisted and turned through coffee plantations and sugar cane farms, then dipped alarmingly into great forests of ebony, sandalwood, cedar, and camphor trees.

Cathy caught her breath at the awesomeness of the tropical rain forest. The fierce light of the noonday sun was all but lost as it filtered down through the mist and foliage to the forest floor. "It's like a magnificent cathedral," she murmured.

Robyn smiled. "You're not the first person to make that comparison. It's an inevitable metaphor—the cool, dim light, the utter stillness, the massive grandeur of the giant trees."

"Can we stop?" she asked, nodding toward a small roadside pull-off.

Robyn glanced at his watch. "Only for a minute. I

want to catch the afternoon flight out of Goroka so we can spend more time at Port Moresby."

Stretching her legs from the long ride, Cathy looked upward through the multistoried canopy. Layers of woody vines—the lianas—plastered themselves against the tree trunks or looped down from the canopy of leaves. They were supplemented by the air plants which perched high up on the branches and trunks of trees, ever reaching for the light.

Ferns, orchids, bromeliads, hanging mosses—it seemed the variety of flora was endless. Following her gaze up the branchless trunk of a tall Cecropia tree to its crowning leafy parasol at the top, Robyn mused, "What was that the poet said? 'Only God can make a tree?'"

Cathy laughed. "Well, He sure did a good job on that one! It's magnificent!" As she brushed against the tree trunk, Robyn suddenly grabbed her wrist and thrust her away from it.

"What on earth?" she exclaimed, rubbing her wrist.

He pointed to a huge ant nest just inches from where she had been leaning. "In the rain forest, you quickly learn to avoid ant-protected trees. If not, the consequences are painful."

She shuddered. "I've heard some horror stories about them—let's go!"

The hot, tropic wind blew through the open Jeep, loosening the strands of Cathy's hair from its tight knot.

"Might as well let it out," Robyn suggested. "There's nobody here but me to admire your beauty, and I have to keep my eyes on the road, more's the pity."

As they rounded a curve, they passed a man sitting on a rock, armed with a bow and a sheaf of arrows. "*Apinun, masta!*" he called to them in pidgin. A short way further on they passed several other men walking along the road, also armed with spears or carrying bows and arrows.

"Are those men hunting?" Cathy asked.

"No, they probably have a tribal score to settle." He nodded toward the highway. "And it looks like the scorekeepers are coming now."

A troop of perhaps twenty or thirty men, some in *laplaps* or loin cloths, and others in jeans and Western-style shirts, marched up the highway, bristling with arms. Overhead they carried a large sign: "The partly payment of the compensational car accident." In smaller print the sign emblazoned the name of the victim and the date of the accident.

Taking in their fierce body and face paintings, warrior headdresses, and spears, Cathy whispered, "Shouldn't we get out of here?"

"Don't you want to stay and watch the fun?" he teased. "The government has cracked down hard on tribal revenge killings. If these guys run true to form, they'll negotiate a settlement in cash and pigs." He went on to explain the swift highlands-style justice. "It's called payback and must be paid even if the death of their clan member was accidental. If they can pin the blame on somebody, it's always good for a few pigs."

"To think I've lived here for six months and didn't learn anything about this country," Cathy lamented, her voice taking on a rather mournful tone.

Robyn reached over and patted her hand. "We're going to remedy that in a hurry. You're traveling with a man who knows this area like the back of his hand!"

"Braggart!"

"No brag, just fact." He smiled broadly. "I really have traveled all over this place, but it's much more interesting when there's someone to see it with me."

Cathy directed her gaze to the farming area they were approaching, trying to hide the blush on her face from those piercing blue eyes. Watching the highland women working patches of *kaukau* with wooden digging sticks, she observed, "Their primitive tools are quite a contrast to the huge machines your company uses."

"Don't let their poor appearance fool you. These highland farmers may look dirt poor, but there's a lot of cash floating around up here, mainly from their coffee crops. Not too long ago one of those guys came down to the mine," he continued. "Wanted to buy a couple of our crawler tractors to use on his farm. He was the real thing—nose plug, *asgras*, and *bilum* bag, and didn't look like he had two *toea* to rub together."

"Did you sell him a tractor?"

Robyn laughed. "He looked over our used equipment and asked how much for three crawlers. He came back half an hour later and emptied his *bilum* bag out on my desk. The exact amount, to the last *toea*."

"How long have you been here?" Cathy asked abruptly.

"Oh, in and out, or back and forth for five or six years. Mostly, I flew in from Australia as a trouble-shooter only when they had problems with the mining equipment. Then when they started winding down the Star Mountain operation a couple of years ago, I moved in with the Ellises to be close by."

"Why didn't you live at the mining camp with the other men?"

Looking thoughtful, he answered slowly, "I did, at first. But after I met the Ellises, and subsequently, the Lord, I decided a mining camp wasn't helping my Christian growth. They get pretty wild at times."

"But you surely must have missed the conveniences of the camp?"

"I guess I did, but the fellowship with the missionaries more than made up for having to shave in cold water. And I learned a lot. Boy, did I learn a lot!"

Cathy raised an eyebrow questioningly. "About religion?"

"Yes, that too. But I also learned about the language,

about myself, and about people. The past two years have been good for me." He chuckled. "Did I tell you about my first real *faux pas* with the local language?"

She nodded her head negatively, and he continued. "I'd just been at the Ellises' a few days when this native came running up, shouting at me to get help. He said some woman had murdered her baby by throwing it down the toilet, so I ran to get Pete. The only thing was, what the guy really tried to tell me was that his sister was sick in the hospital and he wanted a ride in to see her."

"That's marvelous!" Cathy laughed. "Ah, sweet communications. That's almost as bad as some of the things Heidi comes up with."

"You should hear Marva's communication story. She very carefully and distinctly asked one of the native women to pluck a chicken and put it in the refrigerator. When she finished with her patients that afternoon, she opened the refrigerator and found the plucked chicken shivering from its long naked exposure to the cold. She had forgotten to mention that it had to be killed first!"

Together they laughed and talked the hours away and were soon wending their way through Goroka traffic to the airport.

"Are we here already?" Cathy asked incredulously. "It seems like we just left home."

Robyn agreed. "How time flies when you're having fun!" he quoted.

Chapter Ten

Cathy was thrilled by the sight of Port Moresby from the air. Gleaming white high-rise office buildings loomed above tree-shaded streets, and the late afternoon sun drenched the beaches lining the shore. Fields of pineapple and sugar cane yielded to the spires of the gracefully sloping Owen Stanley mountains, and hovering over the entire scene was Mount Victoria, its 13,000-foot peak drawing the eye heavenward.

Robyn collected their baggage at the air terminal and arranged for a rental car. "Well, Princess, what will it be? Shopping, or a night's rest?" he asked as he pulled the small blue vehicle out of the parking area. Without waiting for her answer, he headed northwest on the coast road. "Somehow I think our shopping expedition is going to be an exhausting one. Let's save it for tomorrow."

Cathy studied his strong, firm hands on the wheel. "I'm not that hard to please," she protested quietly, yet strangely relieved. Never in her life had she gone shopping with a man, preferring to order her jeans and shirts from a mail-order catalog.

Robyn turned the car in at a long winding driveway, and they rumbled across an ancient one-lane bridge. A native opened a rope and thatch gate, revealing a cluster of thatched-roof cottages in the style of Tahiti and Fiji. Torch lamps bathed the walkways in a golden yellow glow, and exotic flowers bloomed everywhere. Cathy drew in her breath. "It's the most beautiful place I've ever seen!"

"You like it, then?" Robyn asked, a broad, pleased smile lighting his face. "It's one of the most unusual hideaways New Guinea has to offer, and the food is superb."

After registering, he led her to a garden table in the restaurant, overlooking an emerald, pandanus-fringed lagoon. The riot of color assailed her senses—the flamboyant scarlet of poincianas, the pink and purple bougainvillea, the shimmering emerald water massed with exquisite blue and ivory lotus lilies, and the yellow blossoming cascara trees.

A brightly plumed parrot in a tulip tree screeched a loud welcome, and a fragrance like tropical incense filled the air. Cathy took a deep breath, inhaling the perfume. Was this really happening? Or was she dreaming?

A lavish meal of seafood, fruits, and sago palm was served in so many courses it took the entire evening to dine. In the long interval between courses, Robyn reached across the table and stroked her hands. "They have one speed here—slow. I hope you don't mind?"

In the candlelight, his sapphire eyes were all blue and green and gold jostling fires, playing tricks with her heartbeats. A million pulses hammered in her throat. She had a tremendous impulse to touch his face, to trace its rugged outline with her fingertips. His look of understanding brought the color rushing to her face. To Cathy's relief, their waiter came with the bill, breaking the spell.

"Would you like to walk on the beach?" Robyn asked as they rose from the table.

He reached down and pulled off Cathy's shoes, explaining, "No one wears shoes on a tropical beach.

Barefoot is the only way to go."

They walked in silence along the palm-fringed sands, warm like soft talcum powder underfoot. Balmy ocean breezes fingered her face and hair, and the sound of breaking waves was the sweetest music she had ever heard.

Robyn seemed to read her emotions. "Gets to you, doesn't it? I think this is one of the most peaceful and natural meeting places of land and sea in all the islands."

"It seems like we've stepped centuries back in time," Cathy murmured. "This place is totally unspoiled by anything made of concrete or rising higher than halfway up a coconut tree!"

Robyn stopped walking, slipping his arm around her waist, pulling her close. Moonlight gleamed on his jet black hair with its deep crisp wave, and his eyes were piercing, yet tender. "That's one of the things I like about you," he whispered, brushing the top of her head ever so gently with his lips.

A million sensations whirled up from deep within her, and she fought valiantly to quiet her runaway pulses. "What things?" she murmured, wanting to prolong the magic moment.

"Some people think peace and quiet is a euphemism for boredom. But you're never bored, and you're certainly not boring." He studied her face in the moonlight.

Desperately, she wanted him to kiss her, yet she also felt a passionate resentment, as she summoned all her will power not to capitulate to his obvious attraction.

He suddenly thrust her away from him. "We'd best get back," he said curtly.

Disappointment raged through Cathy's trembling body. She had wanted his kiss, practically invited him to kiss her with her upturned face. And he had wanted to kiss her, too; she knew that.

Then why the sudden coldness? Cathy was oblivious to the beach's delights as they walked in silence back toward the lagoon. Tortured by doubts, her mind whirled. *He's physically attracted to me, but that's all. Knowing my rotten past, he doesn't want to get involved with a person like me."*

Robyn steered her down the path to one of the tiny thatched cottages. "Here's your room for the night, and mine is right across the path if you need me. We'd better turn in and rest up for tomorrow."

Once again, he bent low as if to kiss her, then abruptly drew back. "You sure make it hard on a fellow," he whispered huskily.

"What do you mean?"

Robyn brushed her hair back with his hands, tilting her face toward his. "I mean I intend to keep my promise never to kiss you without an invitation—but it's getting harder and harder to keep that promise!"

He quietly slipped across the path into the darkness, leaving Cathy staring after him in open-mouthed amazement.

Shafts of golden moonlight splashed across her bed, and the perfume of jasmine and night-blooming lilies wafted into the room. Cathy sighed. Could it be happening? Was she really falling in love? She, who had never even entertained a schoolgirl crush? Love was an emotion she hadn't felt capable of giving, and even now was tragically afraid of feeling. But would it be so traumatic to enjoy it for these few weeks, to pretend she was entitled to a normal life?

One thing she knew for certain. She was no longer the same girl Robyn had stumbled in on those few short weeks ago. She had begun to feel again, to laugh, to cry, to care…to live. Like the clusters of moonlit flowers releasing their heavy perfume beneath her window, she was beginning to blossom, to unfold herself to others.

Before climbing into bed, she gave one last look out the window at the dazzling stars, the blazing trail of the Milky Way, and the Southern Cross. "God, if you are up there somewhere, let this feeling last," she begged.

Morning light did nothing to spoil the enchantment of the hideaway. On the contrary, the blazing sun seemed to enhance and deepen the riotous colors. It sparkled iridescent on the blue-winged butterflies and turned the emerald lagoon into an inky mirror which reflected everything around it.

Seemingly unmoved by the tropical enchantment of their surroundings, Robyn met her at the breakfast table, crisp and businesslike. "I'll drop you by a fashion boutique, take care of some business affairs at the company office, then meet you for lunch at twelve sharp. Will that give you enough time?"

Cathy tried to keep the disappointment from showing in her face. "But, I thought...I mean..." her voice trailed off.

He reached in his wallet. "Here's my bank card. Feel free to get anything and everything that you need."

She reached for the card in exasperation. "It's not the money. I need your help. I don't have the slightest idea what to wear for a Christmas holiday in Australia."

"I'm sorry," Robyn apologized. "My silly sisters spend half their time shopping or changing clothes. I just thought it was something women prefer to do alone. I should have known you're different from other women."

Cathy didn't know if that was a slam or a compliment, so she chose to ignore it. In her typical forthright manner, she confessed, "I'm scared to death to shop alone, yet I'd also feel awkward having you along."

Robyn grinned. "Now that is a dilemma. But we don't seem to have any other options, do we? Tell you what—I'll drop you off so you can browse and try things on for a while. I'll come back at eleven to approve your purchases, fair enough?"

She gave a little relieved sigh. "Okay, but can you give me a basic idea of what I'll need?"

Robyn thought for a moment. "It's hot this time of year, so pick up a few light dresses. Since Mother insists we all dress for dinner, better get some elegant dresses, too."

Cathy's eyes widened. "But you said earlier we were just going to get a couple of outfits. I can't let you buy me an entire wardrobe!"

"Why not?" he argued. "It will be worth a year's wages to see my cocoon emerge into a gorgeous butterfly!"

She grimaced. "Clothes might make a difference, but don't expect miracles."

Robyn came close and stroked her cheek. "You are a miracle, my lovely one. A soft, vulnerable miracle!"

Later, leaving her at the boutique door, he squeezed her hand. "Happy shopping!"

She was uncertain whether the thumping of her heart against her breast was caused by Robyn's remark or her fear of entering the boutique. *Probably both*, she thought wryly. Thankful for all the hours she had spent reading Bonnie's fashion magazines, she took a deep breath to calm her nerves and went inside.

A gracious clerk met her at the door. "May I help you?"

"I'm spending the Christmas holiday on a sheep station in the Northern Territory, and I'm not sure what type of clothes to take. Maybe some coordinates?" she asked tentatively.

The clerk eyed her figure critically, then broke into a wide smile. "Underneath those baggy jeans, I'd say you're a perfect size ten."

Cathy spent a delightful hour trying on clothes and was surprised at her own innate sense of quality and style. Finally she selected a stunning black rayon and silk linen suit with a short, boxy jacket, and a white suit in a nubby textured silk. A black and white polka-dot skirt and blouse set in a soft, flowing pongee coordinated perfectly with the other two suits, giving her at least a dozen different outfits. She added still more possibilities with a pair of houndstooth slacks.

To add a little color, she chose a tapestry print dirndl skirt in soft pink, mauve and black, with a matching dusty pink cowl-neck blouse and a popcorn stitched vest. Herringbone pants in a deep plum color looked stunning with the pink blouse and vest, adding even more combinations. White sandals and black pumps were enough in the shoe department.

Robyn arrived just as she was completing her selections, and Cathy felt a stab of apprehension. What if he didn't like her taste? What if she had spent too much? What if she had selected all the wrong things?

She needn't have worried. Robyn looked over her purchases and whistled. "Wow! A woman who not only has elegant taste, but keeps an eye on the budget, too. You're a marvel."

Cathy felt the color rise to her cheeks at his compliment, but that was only the beginning of her embarrassment. The salesclerk gushed, "Mr. Harroway, your wife has impeccable taste. And you should see her in these clothes! She's so tall and regal, a perfect size ten—she could easily be a model."

"But, but…" Cathy flustered, intent on correcting her mistake.

"No but's about it," Robyn interrupted. "A perfect size ten, huh?" He steered her to a pile of designer jeans and pulled out a size eight in several styles.

"I've got jeans," she protested.

"Not in your size, you haven't. Here, you'll need some tops to go with them…and one really knockout dress for the Christmas party the folks throw."

"But I can't let you buy all this," she argued feebly.

Robyn winked at the clerk. "Now what kind of man would deny his wife a pretty new wardrobe? We want your most elegant evening gown."

Cathy shot him a dark look, but Robyn simply grinned and began looking through the gowns. "Here! This is perfect for Christmas!" He held up an exquisite red gown of silk taffeta.

"Just the perfect color and understated elegance that suits you. Will you try it on for me?"

Cathy was startled by the look she saw in his eyes. *Why, he's enjoying this*! she thought happily.

Pulling the lavish material over her slim body, she felt her excitement mounting. She arranged the puffed sleeves just slightly off her shoulders, accenting her long, smooth throat. The elaborate full skirt cinched with a wide cummerbund emphasized her tiny waist. With one deft motion she twisted her hair into a single, lovely coil and dangled it provocatively over her left shoulder. Nervously, she left the fitting room, feeling very unsure of herself.

The warmth in Robyn's eyes engulfed her, and the air was charged with electricity between them. She felt, rather than saw, his fists clenched at his sides as though he were fighting the urge to touch her. She knew the feeling. She, too, was summoning all her will power to keep from rushing into his arms.

Finally, he spoke. "You look fantastic," he murmured huskily. He looked at his watch. "But the clock is striking twelve, Cinderella, so we'd better be on our way." Picking out the plum slacks and pink blouse, he handed the rest of the things to the salesclerk to be wrapped. "She's going to wear this outfit," he explained.

As the clerk went to wrap their purchases, Robyn whispered, "I don't want to seem indecent, but won't you also need some...some...?"

Cathy had never seen him so ill at ease. "Some what?"

"Well, some of those lacy things to wear under these clothes..."

It was Cathy's turn to be flustered. "I already have plenty of lacy things," she confessed. "The uglies were only for the outside!"

Chapter Eleven

The flight from Port Moresby, out across the Coral Sea, over the Arafura Sea, and finally to the airfield at Darwin passed much too swiftly. Cathy immensely enjoyed her time alone with Robyn. It seemed there was nothing they couldn't talk about, nothing she couldn't share with him.

But, she thought fearfully, she wasn't at all ready to meet his parents, his sisters, or his Australian friends. Several times she had asked about them, but on that subject, Robyn was noncommittal. "You'll do fine," he promised. "Don't worry about it."

She couldn't help but worry, however. Would she fit in? Would they like her?

Robyn interrupted her thoughts. "Well, here we are, in the heart of tropical Australia."

She looked about in wonder. The airport was crowded with officials, stockmen, pearlers, and fur and skin traders. Whites, blacks, aborigines, Malays, Chinese, Koepangers, and all possible mixtures in between milled about together, seemingly oblivious to racial differences.

"We're a very democratic society here," Robyn offered. "Since many of our ancestors were ticket-of-leave criminals from England, none of us has much to brag about. A man is known for his own worth, not his ancestry."

Turning to a man in mechanic's clothes, he asked, "Is my plane ready?"

"Yes, Mr. Harroway. All gassed and lubed."

Cathy followed in silence as an attendant wheeled their luggage to a row of hangars and stopped in front of one with HARROWAY painted conspicuously across its doors.

Robyn stepped aside and drew her back out of the way as the Piper Cherokee was wheeled out of the hangar.

"Is your life insurance paid up?" he teased.

Cathy was aghast. "You're flying?"

"Of course. Who else?"

"But...but..." she stammered. "I didn't realize. I mean, your own plane and hangar..."

He shrugged diffidently. "It's just a small one we keep here for convenience. The others are kept at the station."

"You have others?" The words sounded almost like an accusation.

Busy at the controls, Robyn nodded. "Several. A Cessna, another Cherokee, a helicopter..."

Cathy sat in stony silence during takeoff, her anger mounting.

Sensing her sudden coolness, Robyn reached over and touched her arm. "What's wrong?"

She turned to him, her eyes blazing hard yellow glints. "Just how big is this little sheep farm we're going to?"

"A thousand square miles or so. That's why we need the planes."

"You measure it in miles?" Cathy exploded. "You deliberately lied to me! You knew I wouldn't have come if I'd known your people were wealthy!"

Turning to face her, he put the plane on automatic pilot and held her face in his hands. "I didn't lie to you. I would never do that. It's all a matter of relativity. In the North here, a small station is one that includes one or two thousand square miles. Ours is small by Australian standards. I didn't intentionally mislead you."

Cathy studied her fingernails. "When you mentioned a sheep farm, I pictured a Pennsylvania farm of about one hundred acres. I can't even imagine one person owning miles of land!"

He laughed. "We do things in a big way out here! But please don't worry. My family's just plain folks. Dad's probably more ambitious than most, but I think you can handle him." His voice took on a tender, almost pleading tone. "I want them to like you. I want it very much."

The words were spoken casually, but there was nothing casual about the way he was looking at her. His intent gaze never left her eyes, sending tingles of alarm racing along her nerves. She fervently hoped he couldn't hear the sudden pounding of her heart. There was a second of breathless silence as they continued to stare at each other. She wanted to snuggle close in his arms, to caress his face, to keep those dark, burning blue eyes looking at her with their signals of love and tenderness.

Abruptly, she turned away and gazed out the window. This man was having altogether too much effect on her. She must put up some barriers, erect a more solid wall around her emotions. Rummaging through her purse, she lifted out a hairbrush and fiercely brushed the shining masses of black hair. With skilled hands she looped it back from her face and quickly twisted the tresses in a glowing coil at the nape of her neck.

Robyn reached for the pins she had begun to secure it with. "Please don't do that," he pleaded.

His touch sent shivers racing along her spine, but she was determined to fight his spell over her. "If I prefer to wear my hair back, it's no concern of yours."

"You don't have to hide your loveliness out here, Cathy," he promised tenderly. "No one will bother you, I guarantee it. If any man so much as looks at you on my station, he'll have to answer to me."

She continued to pin her hair back into a tight knot, hardening the lines of her face. How could she possibly tell him it was his gaze she was fearful of, his penetrating blue eyes that frightened her so?

Before long Robyn was circling the Cherokee into a landing pattern. Cathy caught her breath at the vast emptiness spread out before them, miles and miles of lush, vital country, vibrantly alive with breast-high luxuriant spear grass.

"The wet's the best possible time of year to show you Harrowood," Robyn explained. "The monsoon rains bring everything to life. The poincianas, tulip trees, and jacarandas all begin to blossom, and the hills are covered with brilliant green, instead of their usual dead brown."

She looked down with fascination at the giant trees, abloom with brilliant splashes of color. The color seemed to blaze toward them as the plane rushed down the landing strip. The hangar roof flashed silver in the tropical sunlight, hurting her eyes. Turning her head away from the glare, her eyes fell on what looked like a small settlement, sunlit and hill-shadowed, nestled in a dense green valley.

Robyn, who had followed her gaze, remarked drolly, "Welcome to Harrowood, the Harroways' place in the sun."

He put down the plane as lightly as a whooping crane gliding into the river flats and taxied to the hangar. Then he led her to a Jeep parked nearby. Opening the door for her, he teased, "Well, are you ready for the grand assault on old Harrowood?"

Cathy studied her nails nervously. "Actually, no."

He gave her a baleful look. "Actually, neither am I."

Cathy's eyes, dark and bewildered, opened wide. "Is it going to be that bad?" she asked in a tiny voice.

Robyn cleared his throat. "Mom is one peach of a lady. You'll like her. But don't let Dad upset you, okay?"

Motoring up the broad driveway, Cathy tried to get her mind off the fast approaching moment when she would meet the formidable Matthew Harroway. She concentrated on the abundance of berries clinging to native trees, the sun slanting through the bauhinias, and the pink and purple bougainvillea climbing along the fences. The profusion of foliage held her spellbound. Robyn, too, was lost deep in his own thoughts, silently steering the Jeep along the curving roadway.

Suddenly the driveway ended in a large blacktopped cul de sac, surrounded by great clumps of pampas and papyrus grasses and spectacular beds of lilies, dahlias and zinnias in every imaginable color. Beyond the plantings, a low stone wall, alive with morning glories and waxy bush orchids, marked the entrance to Harrowood.

Great hanging baskets massed with begonias and geraniums gracefully trailed down the sides of a massive redwood gate, on which an ornate flower design had been chiseled, painted, and oiled. Across the lintel, in old English script, the same artistic designer had chiseled "Harrowood."

Cathy stiffened. Since leaving Darwin, she had steeled herself to expect elegance and wealth, but this was far more than she had even imagined. She stole a glance at Robyn, who had parked the Jeep and was now coming around to open the door for her.

Unaware of her confusion, Robyn opened the gate with a sweeping flourish. "Welcome home, my dear," he teased, bowing low and ushering her through the gate.

Catching a view of the manor house and sloping

lawns inside the gate, she gave a tiny gasp. The house, a charming sprawling clapboard structure, looked like an eighteenth-century colonial inn with its vintage shutters, fluted cornerposts, and spacious sunlit verandahs.

Painted a soft heritage blue with a blue slate roof and white shutters, the house seemed married to its site, as though it had grown up out of the very lawns which surrounded it. They walked up a stone path to the pillared verandah, where a deep mahogany front door created an inviting entrance.

"Like it?" Robyn asked.

She made a wry face. "It's a bit ostentatious for a small farm, isn't it?"

He shrugged. "So it's a little more luxurious than you expected. You'll get used to it."

Cathy doubted that very much. She definitely was not "to the manor born," and it wouldn't take anyone very long to discover just how out of place she was here. When she heard footsteps approaching beyond the door, her panic mounted. She wanted to turn and run, to go back to the seclusion of her New Guinea house. "This is all a mistake," she turned to Robyn, terror in her eyes. "I've got to get out of here."

"Too late," he murmured as the door opened. "Mother! It's so good to see you!"

A lovely woman with the bearing of an aristocrat stood in the entrance hall, her soft smile welcoming them. She hugged Robyn, then held out her hand to Cathy. "We're pleased to have you with us, dear."

Her voice was deep and throaty, with a clipped, educated British accent. Blue-grey waves softly framed her tanned, youthful face above her trim, young-looking figure. Cathy shook hands primly, her voice betraying just a hint of nervousness. "Thank you for inviting me to share your holiday."

A loud, male bellow erupted from inside the house.

"Robyn, is that you? About time! We've been holding dinner."

Entering the house, Cathy saw a tall giant of a man. His skin was burned bronze by the sun and his hair was an unruly shock of grey. His entire appearance was as formidable as she had feared.

He slapped Robyn heartily on the back. "Good to have you home, old chap. But I don't know that a measly two weeks is going to do me any good."

Cathy couldn't help but notice Robyn's glum look, his unenthusiastic response. "I'll help all I can while I'm here, you know that." Changing the subject, he turned to introduce Cathy. "Folks, this is Cathy Litton, the woman I wrote you about. Cathy, my folks, Matt and Ellen Harroway."

Matt Harroway stood back as if to get a better view of her. He surveyed every detail with a critical eye, much as he might check out a prize ewe. An oath preceded his, "Good Lord, she's a big one! A real prim and proper Mary Poppins. Or is she a schoolmarm?"

Cathy's face flamed with anger and embarrassment. Ellen, as if accustomed to mending her husband's fences, tried to redeem the situation. "You'll have to forgive him, dear. Matt's an expert at breaking wild horses, but he has a great deal more trouble controlling his colorful language in the presence of ladies!"

But Matt was not easily put off. "So now I have to watch my tongue in my own house, do I?" he sneered. "I take it you're one of Robyn's missionary friends." He said the words with disgust, almost as if he considered them profane.

Cathy's eyes blazed. Pulling herself up to her full five-foot-nine-inch stature, she said haughtily, "No, I'm not one of Robyn's missionary friends. As a matter of fact, I'm not even a Christian."

Robyn winced as his father held out his hand to Cathy. "For once the boy may be showing some sense. Welcome to Harroway."

She accepted his outstretched hand with a feeling almost of loathing. No wonder Robyn hated to come home.

Ellen interjected tactfully, "Perhaps you and Robyn would like to freshen up a bit before dinner. Rob, show Cathy to her room. I'll have one of the maids bring in your things."

Robyn led her up a wide, winding staircase, stopping in front of an elaborately carved door. "Here's the guest room. Can you be ready in fifteen minutes? As you may have noticed, my father doesn't like to be kept waiting."

"Is he always so rude?" she asked bluntly.

Robyn grimaced. "Not always. Just ninety-nine percent of the time, I guess." With a little wave, he sauntered off, leaving her alone to inspect her room.

Tones of peach and blue combined to give the room a mood of serenity. A massive, antique tester bed dominated center stage, dressed with a soft blue comforter and a hand woven Irish throw. A blue and white oriental rug, urns full of pampas grass, and baskets of greenery added the final elegant touches to the country French decor.

Cathy sighed. She would never get accustomed to such opulence. She trailed her fingers lightly over the rich smoothness of a bedside table. But it sure would be fun to try!

A doe-eyed maid arrived with her luggage, and Cathy hurried to dress for dinner. In no way did she wish to incur the impatient wrath of Mr. Mattthew Harroway.

The filmy softness of her polka dot dress swished about her lithe body. She uncoiled her chignon, arranging the dark tresses in deep, beguiling waves. Applying just a smattering of light makeup and enhancing the golden flecks in her green eyes, she bent to check the results in the mirror. A wry smile pulled at the corners of her mouth.

Schoolmarm? Mary Poppins? She would show him! Her heart pounding madly, she glided down the stairs and into the dining room.

Conversation, which had been flying with reckless abandon around the dining room, came to an abrupt halt when Cathy entered the room.

Robyn quickly rose to pull out a chair for her. His gleaming eyes ranged over her face and shoulders, pausing to watch the rays from the chandelier dancing in highlights on the tips of her silky waves. Intrigued, he whispered, "You look fantastic."

Cathy smiled quickly at him. "Thank you."

Ellen introduced Robyn's three younger sisters, all of them female replicas of Robyn's dark good looks. "And this is our nearest neighbor, Sylvia McConnell," Ellen said, nodding in the direction of a cool, blonde beauty seated on Matt's right hand.

She narrowed her clear blue eyes into tiny, unwelcoming slits. "Pleased to meet you, Miss...uh, Lidden," she purred.

"Sylvia here has been Robyn's sweetheart since they were in diapers," Matt's big voice boomed. "And some day he's going to wise up and announce his intentions, isn't he, love?"

Sylvia playfully ducked his hand as it reached out to pat her hair. It was obvious she knew how to handle the coarse grazier. "Now, Matt," she teased. "You know I only go for Rob because you're already taken."

Robyn made little effort to hide his disgust and attacked his food with a vengeance. Matt and Sylvia continued their foolish banter, almost as if taking pleasure in Robyn's discomfort.

Determined to bring the sparkle back to Robyn's eyes and forgetting her own nervousness, Cathy took the plunge. "On the drive in from the hangar, I couldn't help noticing the quality of wool on some of your sheep. Spanish Merinos, aren't they?"

Matt turned his attention from Sylvia and looked at

Cathy in wonder. "You know about Merinos?"

Cathy laughed modestly. "Not a whole lot. Just that their wool is of superior strength and resilience and that the English woolen mills would go to war to get it!"

Robyn gave her a secret, gratified smile, and soon the conversation swirled around sheep. Matt and Robyn told stories of the kings of Australian workers—the sheep shearers—and tall tales about their highly trained sheep dogs. *Matt seems almost human*, Cathy thought, listening as he warmed to his favorite subject.

"Yes, sir," he bragged. "One of my dogs was so intelligent he learned to play chess."

Robyn, relaxed for the first time since they had entered the house, repeated the old family joke. "Yes, but he turned out to be not quite so smart. I always beat him two games out of three!"

Cathy laughed with delight, her eyes flashing gold in the candlelight. Sylvia gave her a pale, lofty stare as if to say, "You'd better back off—he's mine."

Sylvia yawned, a delicate casual gesture. "We eat, sleep, and breathe sheep around here," she pouted. "Can't we talk about something else for a change?"

Ellen rang for the maid. "I think it would be pleasant to have our coffee on the verandah," she suggested in her impeccable accent. "Shall we?"

As they followed Ellen out to the jasmine-scented verandah, Sylvia quickly jockeyed herself into position next to Robyn. "It's been such a long time, darling, and we have so much to talk about," she gushed, tucking her arm cozily into his.

Cathy stole a glance at the woman Matt had picked to be Robyn's bride. Exquisitely made up and groomed, she looked like one of the models in Bonnie's fashion magazines. With her lithe coordination and casual, inbred elegance, she would be a devastating rival for anyone who happened to fall in love with Robyn.

Watching Sylvia's easy flirtation with Robyn, the coy, lowered eyelids, the graceful movement of her hands, the calculated touches at just the right times, Cathy became strangely angry. *Whatever is Matt thinking about? Sylvia could never make a man like Robyn happy—she's too shallow, too phony*!

Cathy was drawn into more discussions of sheep with Matt and Ellen and found to her surprise she actually enjoyed talking to the older couple. Overlooking Matt's casual profanity, she discovered he was a typical cowboy—an expert on his animals, but ill at ease on any other topic. Much of his coarseness and bellowing was simply a coverup for his insecurity, she thought with rare insight.

Ellen was as well-bred and sophisticated as Matt was coarse and vulgar, proving the old adage that opposites attract. Yet they seemed to be very much in love, and Cathy caught the occasional tender glimpses passing between them.

Later, as Cathy lay in bed rehearsing the day's events, her impressions of Harrowood, and her wonder at being there, she heard a low, soft sound from the garden, a sound like a woman's laughter.

She padded over to the window and pulled back the soft peach drapery. Two figures were strolling arm in arm on the stone path back toward the house. The sound wafted upward again, a ripple of gaiety with inviting overtones. As the couple emerged from the trees into the dappled moonlight, Cathy recognized Robyn's unmistakable tall lean frame. Sylvia was with him, her long golden hair swinging, her glamorous silver satin jumpsuit ghostly in the moonlight.

Silently, Cathy closed the curtain and climbed back into the tester bed. She wasn't jealous. She had no right to be. There was no good reason Robyn shouldn't marry Sylvia, merging their two stations into one gigantic enterprise. No good reason, except Robyn had told her quite emphatically he had no intention of obeying his father's wishes. Perhaps that was it—maybe he really loved the golden blonde, but was still rebelling against Matt.

But hadn't Robyn invited her here to be a sort of protection against both the domineering Matt and Sylvia's appealing wiles? And she was appealing, Cathy had to admit that. Chic, classy—Sylvia would make a terrific prestigious wife for a wealthy station owner.

Turning on her side, Cathy punched at her pillow ferociously. Why must life always be so unfair?

The next morning at breakfast, Robyn announced, "Think I'll ride out and give the place a once-over." Looking toward Cathy, he asked, "Want to come along?"

Torn between a strong desire to see the station and a strange urge to retaliate for Robyn's midnight stroll with Sylvia, Cathy hesitated. Her common sense won out. When would she ever get a better opportunity to see an Australian sheep operation?

As they approached the stables, which housed all sorts of horses, Robyn asked, "What kind of mount do you want—gentle, spirited, or trustworthy?"

She laughed. "Can't I have all three?"

"One trustworthy, gentle spirit, coming right up." He led out a beautiful black filly and prepared to saddle her. "Midnight is gentle as a doe but she can run, in case you want to try life in the fast lane."

When he brought out his own mount, a palomino gelding, Cathy couldn't resist a taunt. "I see you also prefer blondes in your horses."

Robyn raised an eyebrow and asked as he helped her mount Midnight, "Now just what was that supposed to mean?"

Cathy faked an air of indifference. "It just means that some gentlemen prefer blondes—for cozy midnight strolls or early morning rides."

"Sylvia was lonely last night. She just needed some-one to talk to."

"Oh, I'm sure she did."

Robyn swung onto the palomino and turned to look at her. His clear blue eyes held a glint of a smile. "Why, I do believe our visitor is jealous."

She flushed scarlet. "You're out of your mind! But you did bring me along on this holiday to protect you from Miss McConnell's clutches, didn't you?" Before he could answer, she rushed on. "Why is she staying here anyway? Doesn't she just live next door?"

Robyn smothered a laugh. "Next door in the out-back can be five hundred miles away! Her folks are in England visiting the wool markets, so she stays here where there's a little life. Irish Echo can be a pretty lonely place."

"Doesn't she have any other family?"

"Nope. Sylvia's an only child, which accounts for her bratty attitude sometimes. But she's not a bad sort."

Cathy was certain Robyn was a poor judge of Syl-via's character, but decided to drop the issue. "So she stands to inherit the entire station?"

"Irish Echo is the largest sheep and cattle station in the North Territory. Whoever marries Sylvia gets the whole thing," he explained.

"And you're the leading candidate."

Robyn sighed. "According to her folks and my fa-ther, I'm the prime contender, possibly the only one."

"Why don't you marry her then? You could do worse." Even as she spoke, Cathy felt a tug deep in her heart. Somehow the thought of his spending his life with Sylvia upset her more than she would admit.

Instead of answering, Robyn led the way through a field of high grass. They rode a long way in silence. At last Robyn pulled the palomino up. Dismounting, he reined in her mount. "Let's get down for a spell."

With her mind still on other things, her toe caught

in the stirrup, throwing her awkwardly into his arms. Their eyes were mere inches apart. Cathy knew better than to look into those startlingly vivid eyes, yet she couldn't force herself to turn away. It was as though a powerful magnet was holding her, refusing to free her from its strength. She tried to say something, but her voice shook and died in her throat.

Robyn, too, seemed entranced. "To answer your question..." he began slowly.

Cathy frantically searched her memory. *Question? What question? What had they been talking about before the disconcerting spell had been cast over her?*

Robyn continued speaking, choosing his words carefully. "Since I turned my life over to the Lord my entire way of thinking has changed. I couldn't marry any woman, no matter how much I loved her, if she didn't love my Lord and share those values."

Cathy felt her heart would break. So he did love Sylvia—but he wouldn't marry her because she didn't share his religious beliefs. But he couldn't love her very much, Cathy consoled herself, if he would let a little thing like religion keep them apart.

"Let's race," she challenged abruptly, jumping back into the saddle. Activity was what she needed, something to get her mind and heart off the inevitable.

Midnight could indeed run, she discovered happily. Allowing the black filly free rein, Cathy exalted in the delightful sensations of the wind in her hair, the sun on her back, and the fast, rhythmic pounding of the horse's hoofs.

Despite her head start, Robyn soon drew alongside her. "You're some rider," he called.

Basking in the compliment, Cathy teased, "But you caught me!"

Grinning, Robyn muttered softly, "I think it's the other way around."

Cathy slowed Midnight to a walk. "What did you say?"

Robyn looked embarrassed. "Nothing. Here, let me show you around the headquarters."

Slowly they rode through what looked like an entire village. It had barracks, storehouses, machine shops, gardens and small parks, even a service station for fueling the station's many vehicles. Cathy was awed by the immensity of it all. "This is almost a town in itself!" she exclaimed, as Robyn pointed out the workers' residences.

"I guess you could call it that. It takes a lot of people to run an operation like this, and they must have a place to live. And wherever people live, they must have goods and services. How would you like to live way out here with no beautician or barber, for instance?"

Cathy's hands went automatically to her wild, wind-blown locks. "I haven't used a beautician enough that I'd ever miss one," she admitted.

Robyn reached over and flipped her hair with his broad, tanned hand. "You're right! Why would someone as beautiful as you are need a beautician? Anyway," he continued, "the more services we can provide out here, the better quality help we can attract and keep. Some wives hate station life, and that makes it hard to keep good men."

"How could anyone hate it here!" Cathy exclaimed

"Are you applying for a permanent job?"

A becoming flush tinted her cheeks. "I didn't mean...I mean...well, it's just so lovely here...." She finished lamely. Attempting to draw attention from herself, she asked, "Why did you leave all this? Don't you like it here?"

He gazed off toward the bluffs in the distance, apparently deep in thought. "I love this place," he said finally. "Or I would if Dad would get off my back. Going into engineering at the university was my not-so-subtle way of telling him he didn't own my life."

"Matt's not so bad, once you get used to him," Cathy

131

said in defense of the older man.

Robyn shot her a questioning glance. "You're lining up on his side, too?"

"Why do there have to be sides? It's clear you two have a personality clash, but you could try a little harder to understand him."

Robyn grinned. "Now you sound just like my mother!"

"Well, it's true. I think he's gruff and coarse to cover up his lack of culture...."

"Regular little armchair psychologist, aren't you?" Robyn teased. "You're right though. He met my mother in England—she's the daughter of a wealthy woolen mill owner, and he was just a sheep station roustabout. I think he has always felt he wasn't good enough for her."

"But she obviously adores him."

"That's one thing I can say for Dad," Robyn admitted. "He treats Mom like a queen. He practically worships the ground she walks on. She in turn thinks he's the world's greatest. I used to think of them as Beauty and the Beast."

"Maybe he represents a kind of freedom from convention that she needs."

"You really are a psychologist, aren't you?" he teased. "Tell me, how have you analyzed me?"

She grinned, her green eyes sparkling. "You don't want to hear it, do you?"

"Am I that bad?"

Cathy was saved from answering when three kangaroos bounded across the path in front of them. "Oh!" she exclaimed, startled and fascinated at one and the same time. "They're marvelous!"

They watched silently as the strange animals leaped on their powerful hind legs, racing off into the distance at remarkable speeds. When they had disappeared into the tall grass, Cathy asked, "How fast were they traveling?"

Dismounting to stretch his legs, Robyn helped her down. "Oh, they've been clocked at twenty-five to thirty miles per hour," he answered. "They're quite the fascinating creatures."

"Australia is full of fascinating creatures," she commented, a teasing tone in her voice.

"Meaning what?"

"Oh, odd animals like wombats, dingos, the duck-billed platypus, and bandicoots—and you!" she dared.

Without warning, he pulled her close. "So you find me fascinating, do you?"

His eyes met hers; the air was charged like the moment before a tropical storm. Emotions raged deep within Cathy, threatening to engulf her. Her lips quivered with longing for his touch.

Suddenly, he thrust her from him. "We'd best head back for lunch," he said, his voice a raspy breath.

He doesn't even want to touch me, she thought hopelessly. She mounted and reined Midnight around, moving quickly away from him across the grassy savannah. The very sight of him made her pulses pound crazily. She was out of her depth in this strange new world of emotion. Oh, why couldn't she return to her icy state of existence?

But in her glacial limbo she would never have experienced this tantalizing new world either. She had to admit that Robyn had awakened her senses to the beauty and excitement around her. But was it worth the hurt? *Yes, yes, yes*—her heart answered her to the rhythm of Midnight's feet.

Chapter Twelve

Robin drew up beside her, and Cathy automatically slowed her filly. "Those clouds overhead don't exactly look peaceable," Robyn observed, directing her gaze skyward. Near the horizon the sky had taken on a peculiar brassy sheen, ranging from deep apricot to a yellowish tint in front of the ominous cloudbank. The dark mass was moving toward them with terrific speed. Jagged lightning pierced the sky, followed immediately by extraordinary claps of thunder, rumbling from the black cloud formations.

"A big one's brewing," Robyn said. "There's no way we can make it back—follow me." He prodded the palomino into a gallop, scaring up great flocks of birds who were taking shelter in the reed flats.

Cathy followed, urging Midnight to keep up. Great splats of rain began to fall, soaking her hair and clothes. "Hurry, Midnight, hurry!" she begged.

Abruptly Robyn turned into an opening among the casuarinas, revealing an old, dilapidated hut. "Come on," he called. He tied his palomino in the lean-to on the side of the cabin, beckoning for Cathy to follow him.

A close-hitting streak of lightning and its accompanying burst of thunder were all the urging she needed. She jumped from the horse, leading her into the run-down lean-to, then hurried inside the hut.

"Isn't much," Robyn commented. "But at least it's dry." As Cathy explored the tiny shack, Robyn explained, "This was an old sheepherder's cabin." A worn divan filled one end of the room, and a crude handmade table and chair sat before a crumbling fireplace.

He rummaged around the room and shortly found enough burnable rubbish to start a small fire. "Better sit over here and get dry," he invited, pulling the divan closer to the fire.

Cathy shivered. "It's amazing how cold you can feel in the tropics."

"As soaked as we are, we could feel cold in a volcano! Here, let me warm you up." He vigorously massaged her shoulders, with a touch that started the blood racing hot in her veins.

Swiftly, she pulled away. "Thanks, but I think I'm warm enough now."

Robyn eyed her closely. "But you're shivering. You're not still frightened of me, are you?"

She studied the chevron-shaped print on the faded divan before meeting his gaze. "No," she replied honestly. "I'm not afraid of you anymore." To her surprise, she realized it was the truth. A few months ago she would have fled in terror from such a situation.

"You've changed a lot in the past few weeks."

Cathy looked at him intently. "Is that good or bad?"

"All good! I wouldn't have believed the man-hater who nearly banished me to the jungle could have evolved into such a tremendous friend."

She swallowed hard. How could she keep him from guessing that friendship wasn't what she wanted? She stood up, positioning her back to the fire. "Time to dry out the other side." A loud clap of thunder startled her, and she jumped visibly.

"Are you frightened of storms?" he asked.

She bent down and warmed her hands over the embers. "I'm afraid of a lot of things—or at least I used to be."

"What sort of things?"

"Oh, big dogs, the dark—we even had a mean old rooster that used to chase me around the yard."

His laugh filled the small room. "I think all kids are afraid of those things. But we outgrow our fears eventually."

Cathy's huge green eyes studied his face, pleading for understanding. "I'm just now beginning to outgrow some of my phobias," she confessed. "In fact, being in this tiny hut would have been impossible for me before. But now I feel safe, sheltered."

"Claustrophobia?"

She shook her head. "Not really." She lowered her head, as if ashamed. Faltering, she continued, "The only place I could hide away from…from…him…was the dark, dirty outhouse in the farmyard. It was terrifying."

Robyn clenched his fist at the horrors she had suffered. "You know something?" he asked softly. "It makes me feel great to know you trust me enough to share things like that."

She looked up at him in surprise. "I've never, ever told anyone about any of it," she stammered. "Not even Bonnie. I don't know why I feel like telling you. You're the closest thing to a real friend I've ever had."

His face revealed his pleasure at her confidence in him. He turned quickly and walked over to the door. "Storm's still raging," he announced. "We may be here awhile." He went out to the lean-to and came back with an armful of wood. "Might as well be comfortable."

Beginning to dry off, Cathy curled up on the divan, tucking her legs beneath her. Robyn joined her, sitting just close enough for a comfortable conversation. "Those kangaroos were magnificent, weren't they?" she began, recalling the morning's events.

"Technically, those were wallabies," he corrected. "True kangaroos, or wallaroos, are larger."

"Wallaroos, wallabies—why do we call them kangaroos?"

Robyn turned toward her, playfully grasping her hands. "Milady, your Australian history lessons are about to begin. English Captain James Cook, the famous explorer, was captivated by the strange beasts. When he asked the aborigines in English the name of the surprising animal, they answered in their language, '*Can ga ru*,' meaning 'I don't understand.' Cook thought they were answering his question, and they've been kangaroos ever since!"

Cathy laughed, a delightful throaty sound. "Is that the truth!" She leaned her head back on the divan and closed her eyes. They sat in comfortable silence, listening to the crackling fire and the relentless dripping of the rain on the tin roof. "That rain on the roof sounds like popcorn popping," she mused aloud.

Robyn cocked his ear toward the ceiling. "It sure does, but I wish you hadn't mentioned popcorn. My stomach is sending me powerful hunger messages."

"If it doesn't stop growling at me, I'm going to growl back!" Playfully, she jabbed at his abdomen with her doubled-up fist.

Robyn caught her wrist, and the moment his hand touched hers, the air between them was charged as though with the lightning that continually parted the sky. Holding onto her hand, he stroked it tenderly, tracing her fingers from tip to palm. Abruptly and without warning, he raised her hand to his lips and kissed it passionately. She trembled with delight, her pulses racing. He clasped her hand close to his lips. Then, just as suddenly, he dropped her hand and walked over to the fire.

"I'm sorry. I had no right to do that," he apologized huskily.

Cathy, too shaken to reply, simply stared into the

fire. How could a little thing like a kiss on the hand rouse such feelings within her? She, who had always prided herself on keeping her emotions numbed!

After what seemed hours, but was only a few minutes, Robyn broke the silence. "Weren't we talking about popcorn?"

Cathy nodded.

"Did I ever tell you about the first time I took my popcorn popper to the Ellises'?" Without waiting for her answer, he continued. "They invited some of their Bsorio friends over for the occasion. It seems the natives had never witnessed the magic properties of popcorn. They jumped up and down with glee as the kernals pinged against the bulging lid."

She laughed gaily. "I can just picture that scene." Pensively, she added, "We sure take a lot for granted, don't we?"

"That we do," he agreed, and went on to tell her some of the other modern wonders the Ellises had introduced to their native friends.

Suddenly Robyn sat up, alert. "Listen."

Cathy listened intently. "I don't hear anything."

"Right! No more rain popping on the roof. That means the storm is over and we can be home in time for dinner."

"Men! All they can think of is their stomachs!"

"Well, we did miss morning tea, lunch, and afternoon tea."

She laughed again. "You Aussies and your tea times!"

He looked severely at her and shook his finger. "Now don't go making fun of our Australian national institutions," he warned, "or there could be serious consequences."

"Like what?"

He frowned, as if deep in thought on an important issue. "Like refusing you any more of Mother's tea biscuits!"

She drew back in mock horror. "You wouldn't! That would be a fate worse than death!"

They both broke into a fit of giggles, laughing nonsensically over nothing. Robyn reached out and cupped her chin in his hands. "You know something? You're a lot of fun!"

Overcome by his casual touch on her face, she tossed her head provocatively. "Beauty and brains, too! What more could a man want?"

He became pensive, tracing tiny circles on the couch with his fingers. "I can't speak for other men, but there's one other thing I have to have in a woman."

Cathy drew in her breath. Purity? An unspotted past? She was almost afraid to ask. Trying to keep it light, she teased, "What more could you possibly want?"

He looked at her, his eyes serious. "My woman has to be a Christian, to share my love for the Lord."

"Well, that sure takes me out of the running, doesn't it?" she retorted flippantly, heading for the lean-to to saddle Midnight.

The ride back was much slower, as the horses picked their way around water holes and bogged down in the high, wet grass. The sky was still dark and threatening, almost a purplish-chocolate color. An occasional ray of sunshine streaked through the clouds here and there, bathing the earth in an eerie green light.

Cathy felt the mud splashing up on her jeans and shirt, the briers and burrs sticking to her legs. It would feel so good to shower and change into clean, dry clothes.

Robyn, who had been riding behind in silence, pulled his palomino alongside Cathy's horse and pointed to the northern sky. "Look over there."

A spectacular rainbow arched across the heavens, radiating violet, amber, and scarlet hues. It seemed to encircle the station house in the distance, gilding it in soft gold.

"Harrowood. My pot of gold at the end of the rainbow." Robyn spoke the words softly, almost as if talking to himself.

"You love Harrowood, don't you?"

Robyn turned to look at her. "It's my life, my heritage. I didn't realize how much I missed it until now."

"Then why don't you come back?"

He spurred his mount. "I just might someday," he said, as he cantered down the trail.

Cathy rode more slowly, reluctant to take her eyes from the awe-inspiring scene the rainbow had created.

Up ahead Robin had stopped, waiting for her to catch up. As a huge drop of rain splatted on his hat, he held out his hand as if testing the weather. "I think we're in for another gulley washer—better hurry!"

They trotted toward the house as fast as the horses could go in the sloppy mud and matted grasses, while the rain beat upon them in sheets. When they reached the house, Robyn called for one of the workers to stable the horses, and he and Cathy ran onto the verandah. Mud-splattered and disheveled, they entered the French doors, dripping water on the Berber rug. The family, already gathered at the table, looked at them with dismay. Ellen was first to speak, "What on earth? Where have you been?"

Robyn explained that the sudden storm had caught them off guard and they had taken shelter in the shepherd's shanty.

Sylvia interrupted, "I'm sure that must have been very cozy!" She shot Cathy an insolent, haughty look.

Cathy turned away, embarrassed by the implications. "I'd better go change now," she said.

Ellen was immediately by her side. "Why, of course. How thoughtless of us to keep you standing here dripping. You'll catch your death. Go right ahead and change—you and Rob can enjoy a nice, private dinner later."

Evading Sylvia's steely blue eyes, Cathy hurried from the room, eagerly anticipating a hot, stinging shower.

Robyn was waiting for her when she returned to the dining room. True to her word, Ellen had the antique trestle table set for two, complete with a small floral centerpiece and candlelight. Robyn grinned impishly. "I think my dear mother is up to her matchmaking tricks again."

Cathy felt the tell-tale blush creep up her face. "I suppose I should have a snappy comeback, but somehow I can't think of one."

He reached over and squeezed her hand. "I didn't say I disapproved her choice," he reminded her. "But she is a little obvious."

Cathy laughed. "If Ellen has her way, you're a marked man!"

The days at the station sped by quickly, much too quickly for Cathy's liking. She often joined the men riding fences and checking on the flocks each morning following tea. Even Matt seemed impressed by her expertise with sheep. At times, he actually sought her advice, a fact which pleased Cathy immeasurably. She liked the older man, despite his curt, gruff mannerisms. They certainly had a great deal in common, and he seemed to have let up a little in his badgering of Robyn.

The only unpleasantness came from Sylvia's nasty barbs each evening at dinner and her constant disparagement of Cathy's interest in the station.

One morning at breakfast Sylvia remarked, "It's so boring around here, Rob. Let me ride with you today and give Cathy a rest. The poor thing has been working so hard—just see how bedraggled she looks."

Cathy, whose temper had almost reached the boiling point, decided she had a few barbs of her own. "How lovely," she purred in her silkiest voice. "Today we had planned to collect dung specimens and analyze them for disease symptoms. I'm so glad you want to help."

A smile played at the corners of Robyn's mouth, and Matt coughed loudly. Sylvia rose and moved languidly from the table, attempting to look graceful in retreat. "On second thought, maybe I'll pass today. I need to redo my nails and hair anyway."

Later that evening, Ellen came to Cathy's room. "I was beginning to wonder if you had any fight in you," she confessed.

Cathy was chagrined. "I shouldn't have been so nasty—after all, we're both guests in your home."

"Nonsense!" Ellen remonstrated. "Don't apologize. All's fair in love and war, and at this point, I think we may have a little bit of both going on here. Many times I've wanted to reprimand Sylvia for her bad manners toward you, but I hoped you would show a little spunk. I knew you had it in you to fight for your man."

Cathy was confused. How could she tell this gentle but outspoken woman that she had absolutely no intention of fighting for her son or any other man?

Ellen glanced at her watch, an exquisite oval locket hanging from a thin gold chain around her throat. "Time to ring the dinner bell. Now remember what I told you—stand up and fight for your man!" With a graceful wave of her hand, she departed, leaving Cathy staring at the door.

She hastily rearranged her hair, twisting it into one fat braid, with tiny tendrils curling provocatively about her sun-bronzed cheeks. The tropical sun was doing marvelous things with her complexion, giving it a lovely golden glow.

Sylvia was more subdued at dinner that evening, choosing to flatter Matt with her attentions. She only looked in Cathy's direction once, when Robyn announced, "We've been working Cathy too hard, Dad. I think we'll take the day off tomorrow and fly up to Arnhem Land for a little Christmas shopping."

Sylvia pursed her lips. "Christmas shopping in Arnhem Land? Whatever could you buy there?"

She's even pretty when she frowns, Cathy lamented inwardly.

"I can think of lots of things I'd like from the reservation," Robyn's youngest sister, Wendy, enthused. "I love to go up there. You'll like it, Cathy, I know you will!"

"And I have all sorts of things in mind," Robyn promised. "Anybody who wants anything special had better get their lists to ol' Santa tonight," he teased.

The three sisters, accustomed to Robyn's generosity, grinned at each other. "You'll get lists," they promised. "Oh, brother, will you get lists!"

The early morning sun was already blazing across the horizon like a huge bronze shield when Robyn skillfully lifted the Cessna off the runway. Cathy felt the now-familiar twinge in her stomach at takeoff and the thrill of watching the flower-bedecked trees shrink to tiny blobs of color far below.

Not even a hint of haze clouded the bright sky. "Going to be a perfect day," Robyn prophesied.

She nodded agreement, settling back against the leather headrest to enjoy the view. Below, a vast expanse of grassland spread out as far as the eye could see. The immensity of this wild land intrigued her. It seemed that here in the Northern Territory nothing could hem her in or hold her back. She felt free to be whatever she wanted to be.

Robyn was a fascinating tour guide, pointing out areas of interest. Here and there a few old, knobby remains of mountain ranges rose above the lowland basins. He occasionally dropped altitude to give Cathy

143

a better view of a particular lake or river. "Better enjoy the streams while you can," he warned. "The rivers and lakes in this region dry up as soon as the wet ends."

She was so fascinated by Robyn's knowledge of the area, she gasped in surprise when the Gulf of Carpentaria came into view on the far horizon. She gave him an appreciative smile. "For what it's worth, time flies more swiftly when I'm with you than with anyone else!"

Taxiing down the airstrip, Robyn kept his eyes on the controls, but a small smile played on his lips. "Thanks. I kind of like your company, too," he said simply.

Motioning to the crowd of aborigines swarming the airstrip, he groaned. "Oh no—they heard the plane and thought it was the fortnightly supply plane."

"Supply plane?"

"Yes, in the rainy season supplies come in by boat or chartered planes to the outstations. The elderly are here to claim their old-age pensions and the younger wives for their child-endowment payments. They quickly exchange the money for flour, tea, sugar, canned goods, bush knives, tobacco—you name it, the bush supply planes are flying department stores."

Cathy glanced around the empty cargo section of the Cessna. "They're in for a big disappointment, aren't they?"

Robyn grinned. "Not when they see we have cash to buy their crafts!" He reached across to open her door, and quickly they were surrounded by dozens of broad, white-toothed smiles.

"Jimmy Bungaway! How are you, old chap?" Robyn exclaimed, reaching out to shake hands with a bushy-haired native, who appeared to be in his late twenties. Introducing his friend to Cathy, Robyn explained, "Jimmy and I go way back together. We were roommates at boarding school."

Cathy forced her face not to register shock at this news. The incongruity of Robyn attending school with this half-naked, wild-haired aborigine was mind-boggling. Yet here they were, talking like old friends anywhere who had been educated at the same university. Australia certainly was different!

"Jimmy has arranged to give us a tourist's view of Rembarnga country," Robyn told her, steering her toward a mud-spattered Jeep.

Before long they were in the cool stillness of a magnificent rock gallery, where a young boy explained the significance of the various paintings. "Some of these paintings were made long ago on this rock from blood of the ancestors. The giant white snake over there, that was painted by the Mimi people, spirits that live in this rock country and take care of it."

Close by, several other young men sat playing the traditional instruments of Arnhem Land, a six-foot hollowed branch called a *didgeridoo*, and ironbark clapsticks, foot-long pieces of solid wood which produced a sharp ringing sound when struck together. The *didgeridoos* produced a low, vibrating drone, which bathed the cave in a haunting music. Soon, their host broke into song, overcome with enthusiasm.

"This is the traditional way to explain paintings," Robyn whispered to Cathy. "All their paintings are accompanied by dreaming music."

Near the high sandstone escarpment in which the caves were located stood a dozen or so bark huts. Nearby sat several women, busily weaving circular mats and bags from peeled pandanus leaves, dyed with natural root pigments. Inspecting the bags, paintings, beadwork, and gorgeous mats on display, Cathy exclaimed, "They're beautiful! Simply beautiful!"

"This is where our Yuletide shopping begins in earnest," Robyn stated, already making his selections. "Mother and the girls love this stuff."

Turning to Jimmy, he asked, "Do you think we could

find Malangi today? Mom especially wanted one of his paintings."

Enroute to Malangi's campsite, Robyn explained, "He's probably the most famous of all bark painters—one of his bark designs is reproduced on our dollar bill." He pulled a bill from his wallet to demonstrate. "This one depicts funeral rites for a legendary hunter who was killed by a snake at a sacred water hole."

Jimmy enlarged the story. "The picture tells about Gurrumirringu, the first great hunter in our clan. He was preparing some kangaroo meat by the water hole. He failed to look out for the evil spirit snake, which was hiding in a tree near the water. So it came out and bit the hunter."

"Our water holes are very sacred," he continued. "We believe the soul of a child comes from the clan water hole, and to the water hole it returns at death. Our water holes lie at the center of our land and are protected by spirits who show themselves to bad people as huge pythons."

Cathy listened intently to Jimmy's fascinating stories. Yet how could this obviously well-educated man believe such nonsense?

They found Malangi sitting cross-legged under a structure of spreading canvas and corrugated iron. Attended by four wives, he completed a design on flattened eucalyptus bark with paints of ground ocher, charcoal, and clay. He worked with silent intensity, shaping a spear-thrower with bold ocher strokes.

Watching the scene, Robyn whispered to Cathy, "The men dream, paint, hunt, and fish all day. The women tend the children, gather the bush tucker—food—and cook it, and do all the work. And we white folks think we can improve on that?" He tapped her playfully on the tip of her nose.

A reluctant smile curved on her lips. "It's a man's world everywhere, just a bit more obvious here."

"Oh, I wouldn't say that. Who has to go out in all

kinds of weather to mend the fences and care for the herds, while the women stay in the nice, air-conditioned station house?"

She shrugged. "So maybe it's different on a station. But where I come from, it's definitely a man's world."

Robyn motioned to Jimmy, telling him something privately. Jimmy came over to Cathy and suggested that he take her to meet some of the women, while Robyn bargained with Malangi for a painting. Jimmy led her into a nearby bark hut, where several women had apparently gathered for tea. Smiling broadly, one of the women brought Cathy a cup sweetened with sugar and a bit of unleavened bread, hot off the baking coals. As they chatted freely with Jimmy, Cathy was shocked to learn some of these bare-breasted, polygamous wives were also well educated and conversant in world affairs.

Eventually, Robyn appeared in the entranceway. "I've done all my shopping," he announced. "We'd better fly out of here before dark."

Firm handshakes, thanks, and farewells revealed his warm affection for Jimmy as they parted company at the airport. "Come over and spend some time at the station," he invited the aborigine. "It'll be like old times." Somehow, Cathy sensed he truly meant it.

A mauve dusk was settling over the land as they took off. "What a day!" Cathy sighed. "I'll remember this the rest of my life."

He looked at her and smiled, a smile that sent flutters racing through her veins. "I'm sure you will," he agreed. The curious tone in his voice puzzled her.

"What do you mean by that?"

He trailed his finger lightly on her cheek. "You'll see. Christmas is no time for Nosey Rosies." He abruptly changed the subject. "Did you enjoy your teatime with Malangi's women?"

"Immensely. I certainly learned a lot. Those women

are well educated. I don't think I expected that."

"What did you expect?"

Cathy shrugged. "Oh, you know—natives..." She groped for an explanation. "I mean, those women look like natives, but some of them speak like school-teachers. Do you know what I mean? And Jimmy—why does he choose to live in a bark hut and believe those silly superstitions!"

Robyn nodded. "I know—it comes as a surprise to most visitors. But it's their way of life, their ancestral heritage."

"Did you know the fathers still arrange marriages for their children, sometimes even before a child's birth?" Cathy asked. "One of the daughters was having a set-to with her mother this afternoon, protesting her father's choice."

He gave her a doleful look. "I'm afraid that practice isn't confined only to Arnhem Land. Some of our parents like to choose our partners, too."

Remembering Ellen's too-obvious matchmaking efforts, Cathy winced. "Well, you do have a choice, you know."

He gazed pensively out the window. "But they sure can make it hard on a fellow."

"Your mother defied her parents to marry Matt. Surely she won't be too angry with you if you prefer to choose your own bride." She said the words almost angrily.

Robyn spun around to look at her in amazement. "My mother? Who's talking about my mother? I'm just saying that when Jimmy's father arranged his marriage to establish clan ties it was no worse than my dad trying to marry me off to Sylvia to connect our two spreads."

Cathy emitted a tiny "Oh," feeling very defenseless as she slid further down into the Cessna's soft leather seat.

Chapter Thirteen

A vibrant Christmas morning sun slanted through the semi-sheer draperies, bathing her room in a soft apricot glow. Cathy stood before her wardrobe, perplexed. Robyn had said the Harroways traditionally skipped breakfast on Christmas Day in lieu of tea at ten o'clock. The family Christmas dinner was to be served at four on the front verandah. What did one wear for a Christmas dinner in the country?

Back home, the Jordans always bounded out of bed at the crack of dawn, opening gifts while still clad in pajamas and robes. And because Christmas Day was usually a great time for sledding or ice skating, warm slacks and sweaters were the customary apparel for the day's activities. This year would certainly be different!

Her thoughts were interrupted by a soft rap on the door. "May I come in?" Recognizing Ellen's gentle voice, Cathy pulled her robe around her and hurried to open the door.

"I see you're not dressed yet," Robyn's mother observed. "Good!"

She handed Cathy a small, elegantly wrapped package. "I wanted to give you this in private."

Cathy's puzzled look changed to pure wonder as she opened the package, lifting out a stunning jade necklace and earrings. "Oh!" she gasped. "They're exquisite!"

Ellen smiled. "I knew you would like them. The set belonged to my grandmother, and I've been saving it for Robyn's wife."

Cathy nearly dropped the jewels in astonishment. "But you're mistaken...I mean, Robyn and I are only friends. We have no intentions..." she floundered for an explanation.

The older woman reached for the necklace and clasped it around Cathy's neck. "No mistake, my dear. I've seen the way Robyn looks at you. There are some things a mother knows by instinct. You and Robyn are perfect for each other, and this jade is perfect for you. It matches your eyes exactly."

Cathy was still in a state of bewildered shock. "But what about Sylvia?"

Ellen flipped her hand in a dramatic gesture. "Sylvia? That's a pipe dream Matt and Morris McConnell have entertained for years, but it won't work. Sylvia is a lovely girl, but she's not for Robyn."

She pulled Cathy to the deep blue velvet chaise lounge and sat down as if preparing for a heart-to-heart chat. "Rob is very much like his father in many ways," she began. "That's probably why they clash so much. At any rate, he needs a woman who adores him, one who will return his great store of affection."

Nearing panic, Cathy protested, "You know so little about me...my background..." she lowered her eyes. "I'm not worthy of Robyn's love."

"Nonsense! I've also seen the way your eyes light up when he enters the room, how your features soften in his presence. That you love him deeply is blatantly obvious. And that's enough for me!"

Cathy squirmed on the chaise. "Is it that obvious?"

Ellen chuckled. "Yes, dear, I'm afraid it is. But if it makes you feel any better, your love for Robyn is no more obvious than his for you."

"Surely you're mistaken. He practically told me he's in love with Sylvia."

"I told you, a mother knows these things. Trust me."

Unconvinced, Cathy continued to protest. "It's quite impossible anyway. Our backgrounds are too different. I have nothing to offer a man like Robyn."

"We'll let Rob be the judge of that, shall we?" Ellen countered. "No one had more different backgrounds than Matt and I, and my parents vehemently objected to our marriage." Her eyes had a dreamy, faraway look. "But no one could have enjoyed a greater life than we have or a richer love than ours."

She arose from the chaise, signaling the end of the conversation. "So you see, there are absolutely no obstacles love can't conquer."

Cathy sighed. She wanted very much to believe this fairy tale Robyn's mother was spinning, but what did Ellen know about obstacles?

While Cathy pondered in silence, Ellen had taken the liberty of looking through her wardrobe. Turning from the closet, she asked, "May I make a suggestion? This white silk suit is exactly right for today. It would look ravishing with the jade."

"I was thinking of that myself," Cathy agreed. "But won't it be too simple?"

Ellen gave her a conspiratorial smile. "Simple, understated elegance is the look we want. If I know Sylvia, she'll be dressed in some dramatic monstrosity. The contrast will work in your favor, believe me!"

Never in Cathy's life had she dressed to entice a man, nor indeed had she ever wanted to. Until recently, she had never even wanted to please a man. Nevertheless, she followed Ellen's suggestion, slipping into the white silk. She piled her thick dark hair in loose curls atop her head, framing her face with deep, soft waves.

Ellen picked up a perfume bottle from the vanity, spraying it lightly in Cathy's direction. "Perfect!" she exclaimed. "Your hair shows off the earrings beautifully!"

Cathy felt her excitement growing as they descended the stairs and entered the dining room. An elegant tea buffet had been set, complete with holly, boxwood, mistletoe, and red candles. The weather outside might be tropical, but every effort had been made to transform the inside to a traditional English Christmas.

Cathy stole a glance at Sylvia, resplendent in a gold lamé jumpsuit which clung to her voluptuous body like a mermaid's skin. Dozens of tiny gold chains looped about her neck, drawing attention to a deep, plunging neckline which left little to the imagination. Sylvia gave her a cold, lofty stare, her icy blue eyes missing nothing. "New jewelry?"

Cathy's hands went instinctively to the jade necklace. "Yes," she said simply. "A Christmas gift."

She saw Robyn's reflection in the mirror over the buffet. He was standing in the archway, directly under a fragrant bundle of mistletoe. Sylvia was quick to see it, too. She strolled over to him, gracefully twined her arms around his neck, and kissed him possessively. Seeing him in Sylvia's arms released jealousy Cathy hadn't known she was capable of feeling.

When Sylvia finally released him from her clutches, Robyn grinned enigmatically. Holding out his arms in open invitation, he gestured toward the mistletoe. "Any other takers?"

Cathy's pulses raced wildly. Oh, if only she dared! Suddenly overcome with shyness, she tried to ignore him, concentrating instead on filling her plate from the buffet.

Robyn shrugged good naturedly. "Well, if nobody else is going to fall for my rather obvious charms, I may as well eat!" He joined her at the table, giving her a warm, appraising look. "You look good enough to eat!" he whispered.

Certain he could see the erratic pulses in her throat, Cathy tried to forcibly calm them down with her fingertips. Robyn's vivid blue eyes followed the motion, stopping to linger on the jade necklace.

"Grandmother's necklace?" he guessed.

Oh, dear, whatever must he think? Did he know Ellen's resolve to give the jewels to her son's intended wife? Cathy's face flamed with embarrassment. Weakly, she mumbled, "Your mother gave them to me for Christmas."

"Nice choice," he said nonchalantly. "They match your eyes exactly!"

Matt's big voice bellowed from the family room, "Are you going to eat all day or do we get to open our presents sometime?"

"Come on," Robyn urged in a low voice. "We can't keep the Big Man waiting for his toys!"

Festoons of pine branches hung from the rough-sawn ceiling beams; baskets of fragrant pine cones and oranges and potted poinsettias flanked the brick fireplace. A beautifully decorated Christmas tree filled the corner. The room looked much like the homes Cathy had seen decorated for the holidays back in the Pennsylvania mountains. More opulent, certainly, but every bit as traditional—not at all what she had expected for a tropical holiday.

Robyn led her to a deep cushioned wing chair, then pulled an antique rocker alongside. As the rest of the family gathered, Cathy surveyed the room. Ellen definitely had a flair for decorating. Australian primitives were cleverly placed about the room, a mini-print coral wallcovering providing a stunning backdrop for the collection.

Wendy, the youngest of Robyn's sisters, sat at the piano and soon had everyone singing Christmas carols— "Silent Night," "Joy to the World," and "Away in the Manger." Cathy was amazed. This was just like Christmas back home with the Jordans.

Matt handed Robyn a large family Bible, an obvious heirloom. "Here, you can do the honors this year," he said gruffly.

Robyn turned to the Gospel of Luke and read the familiar nativity story. Cathy had heard it before, but never read like this. *He really believes it*, she thought wonderingly. As he laid the Bible back on its resting place, Robyn startled them all. "Do you mind if I pray?"

An awkward silence filled the room, indicating prayer was not an accustomed part of their traditions. Ellen broke the silence. "Yes, dear, please do. I think that would be nice."

Robyn prayed a simple but heartfelt prayer; then pandemonium broke loose as everyone tore into their packages. The floor was soon buried under piles of wrapping paper and ribbon. Everyone had remembered Cathy with a gift, making her really feel like a part of this large, gregarious family group.

Cathy leaned toward Robyn. "I loved the way you read the Christmas story," she began. "It sounded so…so…" she groped for the right word. "So genuine, I guess."

"It is genuine," he said fervently. "Though I'm the only one in this family who thinks so. To the rest of them it's just a traditional part of our ritual, our once-a-year concession to the fact that we're a 'Christian' family."

Cathy drew back at the tone in his voice. "You take this religion thing seriously, don't you?"

Drawing his chair closer, Robyn turned to her, his voice all earnestness. "It's not a religion thing with me, Cathy, it's a personal relationship with the Almighty Creator." His eyes, a dark, burning blue, pleaded with her for understanding.

"Is this a private tête-à-tête, or can anyone join in?" Sylvia pulled up a tufted ottoman and invited herself into their conversation. Virtually ignoring Cathy, she turned all her attention to Robyn.

"I simply adore this gold bracelet you gave me," she gushed. "I'll treasure it always."

Embarrassed, Robyn murmured, "I'm glad you like it. It seemed to suit you."

She gave a husky laugh. "I always was your golden girl, wasn't I?"

Cathy didn't stay to hear his reply. She quietly slipped out of her chair and busied herself exclaiming with Robyn's sisters over their gifts. Inwardly, she seethed. *Golden girl*, indeed! Tarnished brass would be more like it!

When the maid rang the dinner bell, Sylvia again maneuvered herself into position beside Robyn, giving Cathy a triumphant glance over his shoulder. Ellen noticed it, too, and gave Cathy a broad, conspiratorial wink.

In a deliberate, offhand manner, Ellen pulled out one of the birdcage chairs. "Let's see—Cathy, as our special guest, let's seat you here. Hmmm…Robyn, I want you here next to Cathy. Dad and I will take our usual places at the ends of the table. Sylvia, how about you sitting there in the middle between Wendy and Carrie?" Surveying the seating arrangements, Ellen smiled pleasantly. "Perfect!" she exclaimed, and rang for the first course to be brought out to the verandah.

When Cathy finally got up the nerve to glance in Sylvia's direction, she was unprepared for the acid stare she received. The blonde's eyes were like chips of blue ice between narrowed lids, glowering at her with open hatred.

Hastily, Cathy averted her eyes. The only other person who had so openly disliked her was her foster mother, and Cathy was beginning to understand that had been pure and simple jealousy. She shuddered involuntarily. Why did life have to be so complicated? Life had given her so little, why should anyone begrudge the few good times she did have?

Ellen, bubbling and gracious, noticed Cathy's quiet withdrawal from the festivities and doubled her efforts to make Cathy a part of the family. She drew her into every conversation, asking her opinions, explaining family jokes. Soon Cathy was back in the spirit of the holiday, diffidently ignoring the icy blue eyes across the table.

They assembled on the back patio for coffee and champagne, in full view of the pool and fountain. Cathy stood by one of the carved pillars, enjoying the soft, star-sprinkled dusk. In the formal gardens beyond, ghostly silver birches stood sentry over tropical flowers, and the sunset reflected its purple and apricot colors in the fountain.

Cathy sighed. A person could get addicted to this kind of life in a hurry. It seemed a million worlds away from her normal life, taking care of Heidi and Jed. At thought of the children, longing tugged at her heart. How she hoped they were having a pleasant holiday, too!

High, shrill laughter punctured the air. "Look, everybody! Our Robyn is a teetotaler now!" Sylvia, who obviously had drunk too many champagne toasts, stood in the middle of the verandah, mocking and jeering Robyn.

Cathy watched as he pulled away from her. "There are many things worse than not drinking," he said softly. "And one of them is drinking too much!"

"Think you're too good for Sylvia now that you've got religion, don't you?" she jeered, making a passionate lunge for him. She staggered and stumbled, falling awkwardly into Robyn's arms.

"I think you've had enough partying," Robyn told her. "Let me help you to your room." As he bent down to pick up the drunken woman, his cornflower blue eyes met Cathy's green ones across the porch, sending shivers down her spine.

Cathy lingered on the verandah long after everyone else had gone inside. Savoring the beauty of the night, she wanted to capture every sight and sound of this Christmas and store them in her memory. When the bubble burst and she had to return to her ordinary world, she didn't want to forget a single memory of this place.

Robyn stepped from the shadows, a large square package in his arms. "Come with me to the gazebo," he whispered, taking her by the hand and leading her down the path. They crossed a short, curved bridge over a lily pond. The gazebo was a charming Victorian structure reminiscent of the band shells back in Pennsylvania town squares. Cathy leaned casually against a latticework railing, while moonbeams played provocatively on her gleaming hair. The scent of lilies, frangipani, and jasmine was intoxicating to her senses.

Robyn handed her the large package. "Merry Christmas," he said, smiling broadly.

Perplexed, Cathy murmured, "But you already gave me a Christmas present—that lovely gold cross."

"Open it," he persisted eagerly. "Just a little something to insure you'll never forget Harrowood." He steered her into the direct path of the moonlight, as she toyed with the wrapping paper. The paper fell to the floor, revealing a large woven pandamu mat, on which was painted a rainbow arching over a goldengilded Harrowood.

"Oh," she gasped. "Oh."

"Is that all you've got to say?" he teased.

She held the painting toward the moonlight for a closer look. "For the first time in my life, I'm speechless. But how...."

"When Jimmy took you to meet the women, I told Malangi what I wanted him to paint. He's been a guest here at Harrowood, and with his vivid artist's imagination, he quickly recaptured the scene." He gave her a warm look. "Do you like it?"

"Like it? I love it!" she exclaimed. "When I have to leave here, I'll hang it where I'll always be reminded of this place."

Robyn grew somber. "Where do you go from here? After New Guinea, I mean?"

She shrugged, a disconsolate frown on her face. "Who knows? I had applied to the National Sheep Station in Idaho as a researcher just before I came down here with Bonnie and Joel. Maybe they'll still honor my resume."

"You're incredible," he murmured softly. "Someday I hope you get everything you deserve out of life." His lips brushed lightly across Cathy's hair, whether by design or by accident, she couldn't be sure.

Her eyes shimmering, she stared at his handsome, dark face. "These two weeks here at Harrowood are already more than I deserve," she said humbly. "I'll always be grateful to you for making this holiday possible."

Robyn smiled, a broad flash of perfect white teeth. "I'm glad you're having such a good time. I was rather afraid Dad and Sylvia would ruin it for you."

"Quite honestly, I like Matt," she assured him. "Now your 'golden girl' is another story."

"Too bad you two can't be friends. With her the nearest neighbor, we at least have to be sociable."

"She seems determined to resent me. My role as decoy seems to be working, but I'm afraid she's hurt about it."

"Nonsense," he interrupted. "She has no designs on me. This whole idea comes from our fathers."

"Men!" Cathy sputtered angrily. "You can be so obtuse! Anybody with eyes can see she's out to get you!"

Robyn turned away from her, the rigidness of his muscular back making a formidable wall between them, shutting her out. Obviously, he cared more for the intriguing Sylvia than he was willing to admit. He certainly brooked no criticism of her.

"We'd best turn in," he said abruptly. "Tomorrow we celebrate Christmas with all the station hands at the bush picnic race meeting."

They walked back to the house in silence, each deep in private thoughts. Cathy was first to break the uncomfortable quiet. "Thanks again for the beautiful painting. It's the nicest gift I've ever received."

He held open the door of her room for her. "Glad you liked it," he said noncommittally. "Sleep well."

Later she kept hearing his words. Sleep well? She couldn't sleep at all! Drat him anyway! What right did he have to burst into her life, make her love him, then act so casual about it? She pounded her pillow in frustration. Why should she care if he loved Sylvia? Maybe that's what he deserved—an icy blonde statue who only saw him as a means to more wealth!

Cathy tried counting sheep, but each fluffy white ball of wool had a familiar dark, handsome face with vivid cornflower eyes. She gave the pillow another bitter jab. "Well, I'll count Robyns, then," she muttered aloud.

The tropical birds in the garden below her window chirped their wake-up songs long before Cathy was ready to rise. She glanced at the tiny carved ivory alarm clock on the bedside table. She'd have to hustle! Ellen had said they needed an early start today.

By the time Cathy showered and dried her hair, neighbors were already entering the gate, preparing for one of the outback's rare social occasions, the annual bush picnic races. Long tables were set up on the lawns, several planes circled the landing strip, and a number of trucks pulling horse trailers were lining up near the corrals.

Hastily dressing in jeans and a plaid Western shirt, she pulled on the riding boots Wendy had loaned her. Cathy loved to ride, and no concerns about who Robyn loved or didn't love were going to spoil her day.

She had learned a long time ago to get through each day as it came, and this was one day she intended to enjoy to the fullest.

She glanced out toward the lawns again. She hadn't seen this many people in one place since leaving Pennsylvania. *At least not English-speaking people*, she thought ruefully.

"The first heats are men's," Robyn said, coming across the lawn to greet her. "But you can saddle up Midnight and enter her in as many events as you want. I already told the stable hands she's yours for today."

Cathy tossed him a grateful smile. He knew how she loved to give the filly free rein, how she and Midnight seemed to sense each other's moves. Her smile quickly faded when she arrived at the stables. Sylvia, in beige jodhpurs and a beige silk shirt, was arguing with the stable boy. "I don't care what Robyn said," she fumed, "I want the black filly saddled right now!"

"It's all right," Cathy spoke softly to the frightened boy. "Robyn told you to saddle Midnight for me, and I'm here now to get her." She looked at Sylvia, as if daring her to interfere. "I'm sure Miss McConnell will select another horse."

Sylvia returned her stare with a withering look. "Now that you've convinced Rob to save the best mount for you, I get to choose from what's left, is that it?"

Mounted on Midnight, Cathy waved her hand and rode out of the corral. No one, but no one, was going to ruin her day.

She joined Wendy and Carrie in the field, where the first heats were already in progress. In the distance, she could see Robyn's palomino closing the gap on a beautiful grey Arabian. "That's Dad!" Wendy yelled. "They're running a close heat!"

The two were clearly ahead of the field and excitement rose as they entered the home stretch neck and neck. Cathy found herself yelling hysterically, "Come

160

on, Robyn, come on!" The palomino gave a sudden lunge, nosing out the Arabian at the finish line. "Oh dear, Matt's going to be angry," she said aloud.

Wendy laughed gaily. "That's all you know. There's nothing Dad likes better than getting beat fair and square by Robyn."

Cathy pondered that bit of information in silence. She'd have to put it on the back burner for some armchair psychoanalysis at a quieter time.

The morning passed swiftly, with Cathy and the girls entering several of the events. True to form, Midnight ran a good race, but she was no match for the racing thoroughbred from a neighboring station. Not conditioned to winning, Cathy really didn't mind. For her it was enough to be part of the action, to feel the wind in her hair, and to see Robyn's glow of approval.

Lunch was a hilarious affair, much like the PTA potlucks back home, Cathy thought. But for these folks, for whom distance made frequent socializing nearly impossible, it was a rare treat, and everyone seemed to be in the spirit of the occasion.

Cathy noticed that most of the graziers, cow cockies, and station hands were much like Matt—rough talking, coarse, gruff, as if a hint of manners would somehow destroy their masculinity. Robyn, who had spent his entire life in this environment, was so gentle and kind, and yet somehow it seemed he was more ruggedly masculine than any of them. She would take Robyn's brand of maleness any day, that was for sure.

Robyn joined her in the lunch line, introducing her to friends from as far away as Alice Springs.

"It seems the entire North Territory is here," she remarked.

The "neighbor" laughed. "More like the whole outback!"

Cathy had to pay close attention to conversations, because even though everyone spoke English, it sounded like a foreign language. Robyn tried to help her keep pace with the fast-flying terms. "Down here we call a buckaroo a ringer," he explained. "Your bronco-buster is our buck-jumper, and the roundup is a muster. Comprendé?"

She laughed with delight. "Clear as mud," she giggled. "Australian mud!"

After lunch, Robyn encouraged her to enter the barrel races. "It'll be a cinch, the way you and that horse understand each other."

To her amazement, she won the event, finishing several seconds ahead of the nearest contender. The flush of victory on her face, her hair curling flirtatiously in the wind, she made an altogether beguiling picture. The black horse and its beautiful dark-haired rider were fast becoming the main topic of conversation.

"Wherever did Rob find her?" "I hear she's an American." "She can really ride." "What a beauty!" Such comments were heard frequently throughout the day, causing Ellen to smile smugly. Her Robyn had good taste!

Robyn's good taste was lauded even more when Cathy made her entrance at the Christmas banquet that evening. Gowned in the red silk taffeta, her hair curled in huge bouncing swirls, she was the picture of elegance. Robyn's tiny gold cross was the only adornment around her smooth, graceful neck.

Robyn strolled over to the verandah to greet her, himself a study in good looks. "Shall we?" he invited, offering his arm for a promenade through the crowd.

Walking with a man who exuded male attraction with every breath, the heady perfume of the garden, the dazzling fountain lights—together they worked some kind of Christmas magic, bringing Cathy to glittering life. Her hair and skin sparkled, golden flecks glowed in her green eyes, and her personality bubbled. Clearly the belle of the ball, Cathy had never experienced such a delightful evening.

Sylvia watched her cautiously, with narrow-eyed, summing-up glances. When Cathy finally moved away from Robyn and headed in the direction of the powder room, Sylvia followed her. "Don't you think you may be overdoing it a bit?" she asked caustically.

Cathy raised an eyebrow. "Overdoing what?"

"Your rather obvious play for Robyn," she sneered. "But I'm warning you, it won't work! He's mine, and I mean to have him."

Cathy looked at herself in the mirror, relieved to see her face reflecting much more confidence than she felt. "Isn't that Robyn's decision to make?"

"No, it isn't. Robyn and I are a long-time enterprise. His father and mine have had it set for years, and I don't intend to let you come in and spoil it now."

Cathy recoiled, unbelievably angry. "An enterprise?" she exploded. "Is that all Robyn means to you? A business merger? You don't even love him."

"And I suppose you do?" Sylvia hissed. "You poor, naive innocent. Love doesn't last two weeks out here in this God-forsaken country. Land and wealth are the only things that count."

Cathy brushed past her, too furious to speak. Her face was still flushed when Robyn found her in the garden moments later. "What happened? You look like you've been in a knock-down fight."

"You might call it that," Cathy answered glumly, the sparkle all but gone from her evening. Remembering his reaction the last time she criticized Sylvia, she wasn't about to make the same mistake twice.

"Can we go somewhere and talk?" he asked. "These crowds suffocate me." He steered her toward a white iron seat on the dark side of the house.

Stroking a wayward curl, he gave her a look that sent her senses reeling. "It's hard to believe you're the same person I met such a short time ago," he said huskily. "You've emerged into a beautiful woman."

Trying to evade the warmth in his eyes, and to cool

163

down her own runaway emotions, she made a weak attempt at humor. "Beauty is only skin deep, but ugly goes clear to the bone."

Robyn traced her cheekbone with his fingertips. "You don't have any uglies anywhere."

She panicked. "But I do," she insisted. "I feel like Cinderella here—all too soon the clock will strike midnight, and I'll be left holding a pumpkin. Life has never been very good to me, and I'm not naive enough to think things are going to change now."

He turned to face her squarely, his eyes full of eagerness. "But things can change, Cathy. Maybe life has hurt you, but there's One who can give you a whole new start in life, One who wants to love you and be your friend always."

Cathy's eyes grew bright with wonder. Could it be true? Was he offering her his love? She murmured, "And who is it who wants to love me?"

"Jesus Christ," he said earnestly. "Won't you…?"

Pain shot through her like a knife. She didn't hear what else he had to say. Jesus Christ? Robyn was offering her religion, not himself. How could he bring her out here to preach to her! A bitter laugh made an explosive sound in her throat. "You never give up, do you?" she asked.

She heard his sharp intake of breath and felt rather than saw the slump of his shoulders. "Sorry," he muttered, as he walked away.

She almost collapsed with the relief of his leaving, pressing her eyes tightly shut to prevent the tears that were on the verge of spilling. She hurried up the back stairs to her room, where she could let the tears flow in privacy.

Chapter Fourteen

Robyn was friendly but aloof during the remainder of her stay at Harrowood. The warmth in his glances was gone, replaced by a bleak, remote hardness. Cathy puzzled over the hurtful change in their relationship. They were together just as often, and he was always polite and gentle, but something important was missing—something she couldn't quite identify, but missed dreadfully.

To worsen matters, Ellen sensed the growing tension between them and stepped up her matchmaking efforts. Realizing time was growing short, she threw them together at every opportunity, making up excuses for them to run errands and engineering seating arrangements to ensure they were always side by side. Times alone were especially awkward, with neither of them having much to say. Their casual, easy-going camaraderie had vanished, leaving in its place strained attempts at polite conversation.

Sylvia, usually quick to spot an advantage, seemed to withdraw also, a maneuver that puzzled Cathy. Maybe she had decided not to buck Ellen's all-out efforts, preferring to bide her time till Cathy was only a memory of the past.

She should worry, Cathy thought bitterly. *The way*

Robyn feels about me, I'm certainly no competition for her merger plans!

On the night before Cathy and Robyn were to fly back to Goroka she stood in the flower-shrouded gazebo, savoring the heavy tropical perfume released by the evening's dew. Breathing deeply, as if to drink in every possible bit of fragrance, she sighed. *Wouldn't it be marvelous to be a part of this always...to belong here?*

For as long as she could remember, Cathy had felt a desperate loneliness, an emptiness, an ache to truly belong to a family. She choked back a sob. No sense spending time on wishful thinking. She would never be more than a guest at Harrowood.

"Well, Cinderella, the clock is about to strike midnight for you." Sylvia's voice intruded into the evening's magic, soft and lilting, yet dripping sarcasm.

Cathy whirled in the direction of the voice. She fought for composure. "We'll be leaving early tomorrow morning, if that's what you mean."

Sylvia's voice took on an even sweeter tone, as if she could afford to be condescending. "You'll be leaving tomorrow," she corrected. "Robyn is merely flying you to New Guinea." She paused for effect. "Then he's coming right back here to me."

Shock registered in Cathy's face, despite her efforts to conceal it. It couldn't be true.

Sylvia's voice again dripped honey and sugar as she said in mock surprise, "You mean you didn't know? I thought surely Rob would have told you."

Cathy struggled for control. The words choking in her throat, she muttered, "I hope you'll be very happy. Now if you'll excuse me, I have to finish packing."

Sylvia caught her wrist, an odd, compassionate look on her face. "You do care for him, don't you?"

Cathy averted her eyes. "Yes," she whispered.

For the first time since they had met, Sylvia's voice

166

softened, its tone almost friendly. "I guess I've been a real witch," she apologized. "When Robyn first wrote and told us he was bringing a woman home with him, Matt and I tried to peg you."

Cathy lifted her eyes. "Peg me?"

"Figure you out. I guessed you were a fortune hunter, out to steal my future. And Matt was certain you were one of those religious fanatics wanting to ensnare Robyn into some idealistic missionary endeavor."

"Bad guesses, both of them," Cathy murmured. "I thought Robyn was a poor sheep farmer until I came here, and religion definitely isn't my thing."

"So we were both wrong. Anyway, that's why we've been so nasty to you." Sylvia laughed, a wry-sounding tinkle. "Not that it changes anything—I still aim to marry Robyn. It just makes it harder, knowing you're going to get hurt."

"I'll survive," Cathy muttered. "I always have." She started up the pathway, but Sylvia again blocked her passage.

"Please try to understand," she pleaded. "I'm not the awful person you think I am—but Rob and I are a life-long dream, and I'd do anything to keep from losing that dream!" She hesitated, then added, "For some reason, I care what you think of me—I want you to like me."

Cathy choked back a sob. "Just be good to Robyn, okay?" She brushed past Sylvia and ran breathlessly up to her room. It was too early to go to bed, yet she couldn't force herself to go back down to join the family. The tears were too close to the surface, her emotions too ragged. She would probably burst into tears at the slightest provocation, making an utter fool of herself.

Yet if she didn't go down, they would think her terribly ungrateful and rude. At times like these, she almost wished she believed in God—someone to call on for help.

A slight rap on the door startled her. "Who's there?"

"It's me," Ellen called softly. "May I come in?"

Cathy went to open the door, trying to rub the tear smudges from her face as she did so.

Ellen eyed her sympathetically. "Leaving is difficult, isn't it?"

Cathy sniffled. "Just having a little emotional waterworks. I'll be all right in a minute." She pressed a handkerchief hard against her eyes, as if the pressure would halt the tear flow.

"Forgive me if I seem a meddling old woman," Ellen began. "But have you and Robyn had a spat? You both seem so unhappy."

How could she make this woman understand? "I wish it were a lovers' quarrel," she sniffled. "But we're not lovers. We've never been anything but good friends."

"Then why the tears?"

Cathy walked restlessly about the room, twisting the handkerchief in her fingers. "Maybe because I wish it could be more, and it's impossible."

"Impossible?"

"It takes more than one person in love to make a romance."

Ellen gave her a strange, inquiring look. "Are you telling me you don't love Robyn?"

Cathy's tear-brimmed eyes widened with incredulity. "I love him with every fiber of my being! But he's going to marry Sylvia." She choked back a sob and headed for the jewelry box on the dressing table.

Taking out the jade jewelry, she handed it to Ellen with a sad little gesture. "I can't keep these. I know you intended these for Robyn's bride, and I'm afraid I accepted them under false pretenses..." her voice broke, and she fell across the bed, crying softly.

"Poppycock! I gave you those jewels because Robyn is obviously in love with you. Believe me, I know my son."

Hope sprang up momentarily in Cathy's heart, but then she sagged back on the bed. "No, it's useless. He as much as told me the only reason he hasn't already married Sylvia is that she doesn't share his religious beliefs."

Ellen sat in silence, deep in thought. "I can't believe he said that," she mused aloud. "That just doesn't sound like Rob. He had plenty of opportunity to marry her long before he got on this 'religious kick' as Matt calls it. No, I know my Robyn, and he isn't in love with Sylvia. She just isn't his type."

Cathy smiled ruefully through her tears. "I'm hardly his type either. Has he ever told you anything about my background?"

"He mentioned you had an unhappy childhood. But things like social status or background don't mean a whit to Rob—he's much deeper than that."

"Like you?" Cathy ventured shyly.

The older woman smiled, a beautiful smile that wrapped Cathy in warmth. "Yes, like me," she agreed. "I never could understand why my parents were so intent on wealth and position, when Matt was such a solid gold character!"

Cathy gave her a wistful smile. "I'd give anything to share in a rich love like you and Matt have. It shows even when you talk about each other."

Ellen beamed. "Marry Robyn and you'll have a love like ours!"

"He has to ask me first," Cathy reminded her gently. "And if all your matchmaking tricks haven't worked by now, I don't think they're going to."

Ellen smiled ruefully.

Cathy gave her a quick hug. "Seriously, I do think you should keep the jade."

169

Ellen finally acquiesced. "All right. I'll take care of it for you. But, mind you, it's only temporary—you get the set back on your wedding day." She headed for the door, suggesting over her shoulder, "Why don't you pamper yourself with a luxurious bubble bath and an early bedtime? I'll give your regrets to the others."

Early the next morning, Cathy and Robyn drove out to the hangar in silence, an uncomfortable heaviness in the air between them. As the plane lifted off the runway, taking her away from this land of enchantment, Cathy twisted in her seat, attempting to permanently engrave every last image of Harrowood in her mind.

The wind rushed along the wing, the surge forcing Cathy tightly against the back of the seat. The vast landscape sprawled out before them, a magnificent checkerboard of green and brooding ocher plains. The nose lifted and they climbed at full power into the blue heavens. For the first time, Robyn spoke. "Beautiful from the air, isn't it?" Pride of possession vibrated in the rich timbre of his voice.

She nodded. "And from the ground, and at night, and in the sunlight..."

"You fell in love with Harrowood, didn't you?"

She nodded again, unable to trust her voice. The lump in her throat was growing, making speech virtually impossible.

Robyn cleared his throat as if preparing to say something, then again fell silent. Finally, not looking at her, he spoke. "I'm coming back to Harrowood."

She nodded. "I know."

He turned to gaze directly at her. "I mean I'm coming back immediately."

She brushed a tear from her eye, hoping he hadn't seen it, and nodded again. "I know," she repeated.

"You know?"

"Sylvia told me last night."

He banged his fist hard against the instrument panel.

"I should have told you earlier."

"You don't owe me any explanations."

He stared intently out the windshield momentarily, then turned back to her. "I don't want our friendship to end this way, Cathy, with hard feelings between us."

She swallowed hard. "What difference does it make? We'll probably never see each other again."

"But I value our friendship. I care about you."

Her eyes brimming with tears, she turned away. Sure, he cared about her. He cared so much he was going back to Sylvia! She stifled a sob, fighting desperately for control. She wasn't going to cry over any man, she told herself. None of them were worth her tears.

Robyn reached over and placed his arm comfortingly around her shoulder. She had to fight the urge to snuggle close against him.

"Please don't cry," he said, his voice full of compassion.

"I'm not crying," she sniffed, pulling away from him. "Just leave me alone."

He stiffened, then turned his attention to piloting the plane. Her eyes shifted from the scenery below to the instrument panels, then to his hands on the controls. Lean and brown and beautifully shaped—strong, responsible hands. Hands a woman could safely trust herself to.

With sheer force of willpower, she made herself look away and out the window. She must blot Robyn out of her mind forever. Dismally, she watched the ever-changing landscape below, the flat, featureless plains, the silver billabongs strung out along the river.

The ground seemed to rise up to meet them as Robyn prepared for the approach to the runway at Darwin. They lost altitude fast, homing in like a giant bird, flaps extended, coming into the final glide. In silence they put down, taxied the Cherokee into the hangar, and caught a commercial flight back to New Guinea.

Seated directly behind the bulkhead, Cathy put her headphones on and tuned into a mood music channel, effectively blotting out any attempted conversation. Again, she fixed her attention on the passing landscape, on the hundreds of offshore islands that ringed the giant reptile-shaped land of New Guinea sprawling directly above Australia.

She marveled at the tremendous contrasts of this wild country—breaking over deep green rain forests, then hovering above the Astrolabe Range where the grass moved in waves like a windswept sea, its color changing from bright to dull gold in the sunlight. In the distance, she caught a glimpse of the Owen Stanley Mountains topped by great banks of clouds.

The contrasting scenery reminded Cathy of her own emotions—and the great fun and high hopes they had enjoyed on the way to Harrowood. By contrast, this return trip was sheer agony, a kind of extended slow torture.

Every glance at Robyn's taut face was an ordeal, every memory of Sylvia like a knife cutting deep into her heart. How she wished she could go back to emotional limbo again, that never-never land of numbness where there was no joy, but neither was there a stabbing ache in her heart.

At Goroka they picked up Robyn's Jeep at the airport and headed back out the Highlands Highway. Finally breaking the oppressive silence, Robyn asked, "Hungry?"

She shook her head. "No."

A reluctant smile curved his lips. "Now that's what I call a fascinating conversation."

She returned his grin with a wan smile. "So what's there to talk about?"

"We never ran out of subjects before. Surely we

could think of something."

Oh yes, she thought ruefully. *We could talk about your upcoming marriage, about your land merger with the McConnells' Irish Echo—all sorts of interesting subjects.* Instead, she lowered her eyelids. "I rather like the silence, if you don't mind."

A look of pain crossed his face as he muttered, "If that's the way you want it."

The silence lay thick and heavy between them as they drove through the great forests of ebony and sandalwood. Knowing every mile brought them closer to the inevitable parting, Cathy tried to quell the panic in her soul. The fact that he belonged to someone else didn't lessen his devastating physical vibrancy, and his nearness threatened to overpower her.

What if she were to take Ellen's advice and fight for her man? What if she were to suddenly throw herself into his arms, confessing her love for him? The absurdity of the thought brought a wry smile to her lips.

Fighting for a man was not her style, would never be her style. No, if he didn't want her, that was simply another of life's rotten deals. Thus fortified, she decided she was prepared for the final good-byes.

Finally they arrived at the mining camp. Robyn declined Bonnie's invitation to stay for supper, explaining he needed to get on to the mine. Watching Heidi and Jed clinging tearfully to "Uncle Rob," Cathy thought her heart would break. If this pain was love, she didn't need it!

Robyn took her hand, his intent blue stare going through her like a shock. "Well, so long," he said huskily.

Her own good-bye was stilted and barely polite, the words coming out with great difficulty. Every muscle in her body craved to cling to his Jeep, to prevent his leaving. Yet with a massive surge of willpower, she turned away from him and went into the house.

"Are we ever glad you're back!" Bonnie exclaimed, as Cathy began to unpack her things.

"Did the kids miss me?"

"Miss you? All I heard was 'Aunt Cathy does it this way,' or 'Aunt Cathy always plays with us!'" Bonnie laughed. "You've sure got them spoiled. I don't think I can ever live up to your image as a mother."

Cathy winced, bending low over her luggage to keep Bonnie from seeing the pain on her face.

"Anyway," Bonnie continued, "Malay authorities have just made contact with a primitive nomadic tribe in the Malaysian jungle. They have had no previous contact with outsiders! Can you imagine what this means to Joel's project?"

Cathy couldn't imagine, but she sensed it somehow included a change of plans. "So what does it mean?"

"Total isolation from outside sources, an uncontaminated dialect! It's a fantastic opportunity, Cathy."

Cathy looked up from her unpacking. "I'm not sure I understand...."

"We've received special permission to tape their language and study it. Probably the last unknown dialect on earth!" She looked thoughtfully at Cathy, before adding slowly, "But it will mean some changes...."

Here it comes, Cathy thought wryly. "Like what?"

"Like Joel and I are to meet the tribe's representatives at Long Marong on the River Tutoh south of Marudi as soon as possible; then it's another day's journey to their village about eighty miles into the interior. So we can't possibly take the kids."

"Slow down, you're talking Greek," Cathy complained. "I've never heard of any of those places around here."

"You're not listening!" Bonnie admonished. "I said in the Malaysian jungle—it's in Borneo."

"Borneo? We're going to Borneo?"

Bonnie shot her an exasperated look. "Joel and I are

174

going to Borneo for several months. We've arranged for you and the kids to stay with the Ellises up in the Bsorio village."

Cathy digested this unwelcome bit of information. "Just like that, without consulting me, all the arrangements have been made?"

Bonnie half-apologized. "Well, it all happened so fast, and it wasn't as though you were here where we could talk it over. I was sure you wouldn't mind."

Capitulating as always, Cathy offered one more objection. "Why can't I just stay here with the children? It's a lot more comfortable and convenient."

"Joel says it's too long to leave you alone. Besides, the government has warned there's another rash of '*fashion bilong pait*' outbreaks, so things are rather shaky around here right now."

Cathy struggled with the unfamiliar term. "*Fashion bilong pait?*"

"You know—the old highlands-style justice system. Several tribes are already shooting it out, and the local authorities have declared a state of emergency."

Cathy shuddered. "You mean they're at war?"

"Not exactly. Just settling tribal scores, but these outbursts can explode sometimes." Bonnie smiled wanly. "Now that you're nearly unpacked, you'd better pack up what you'll need for a few months at the Ellises'. We'll keep the houses here locked up, so you can come back for other things you need later."

The drive back up the Highlands Highway the next morning was like a roller coaster ride in slow motion. The highway was crowded with lazy pigs and countless natives walking up and down, slowing Joel's progress considerably. At one point he had to stop alongside the highway to make room for a parade of dancing girls in grass skirts and painted faces.

Cathy didn't mind the interruptions. She was in no hurry to move into her new quarters near the Ellises.

Bonnie had assured her she would have her own thatched house, already cleaned and made ready by Marva Ellis. Still, she didn't like living in such close proximity to Robyn's good friends. They were sure to ask questions and raise problems she would rather not discuss.

The sun was just starting to set beyond the ridge when they reached the unpaved road into the Bsorio village. Watching Joel struggle to keep the vehicle between the deep, narrow ruts, Cathy surmised neither she nor the Ellises would be navigating this road frequently. Apparently, she was stuck in the tribal village until the rainy season was over.

As they entered the village, Foroba and Bate came running over to their car. Cathy greeted them warmly, glad to see friendly, familiar faces. Bate still wore the shiny gold cross pendant Cathy had given her, still held her left hand out of sight, and had the sad, faraway look in her eyes.

Marva and Pete helped Cathy settle into her new home, a miniature replica of their own home. With her own things spread about the tiny room, it looked almost homey, and she decided life in the Bsorio village would not be totally unpleasant.

Early on, she had let the Ellises know that Robyn was a subject she wouldn't discuss, and they were gracious about her feelings.

With the three Ellis children for constant companions, Jed and Heidi were much less demanding of her time, freeing Cathy to indulge in her own pursuits. She and Marva became good friends. Before long she was busily helping the older woman with her many chores, teaching sanitation and health measures, telling children's stories, and helping with the medical supplies.

Busily involved with the problems of others, she had little time to brood over her own unhappy state of affairs, though thoughts of Robyn and Sylvia occasionally crowded into her mind. Were they married yet? Was he happy? Many times she wanted to ask Marva if they had heard from Robyn, but her own self-imposed silence on the subject prevented it.

Soon Cathy and the children were accepted by the Bsorios. With Foroba and Bate's help, it wasn't hard to make friends among the natives. The tribal people were dependent upon each other, working and sharing together, and soon Cathy was considered just another one of the community. They borrowed from her, exchanged gossip freely, and always had time to admire the children.

The gregarious Heidi was a big factor in their easy acceptance in the village, never meeting a stranger. One day several men were squatting over to examine a kerosene lamp that wasn't working. Unable to see what was going on, Heidi hopped on the village leader's back for a closer look.

Cathy held her breath, waiting for his reaction. The short leader, a flat bone ring in his nose, beamed a broad smile through his scrubby beard. Standing up cautiously so he wouldn't disturb his "rider," he treated the giggling Heidi to a piggyback ride.

The Bsorios loved theatrical performances, a fact that both the government and the missionaries took great advantage of. The Raun Raun Theatre, a troupe of actors from all over Papua New Guinea, often came to educate the villagers on health and sanitation. Cathy found herself as enthralled with these interruptions in the daily routine as the natives were.

The theatrics were a vital part of local wedding ceremonies, with the public part of the wedding including night-long singing at the woman's house. At this sing, the clans of the betrothed couple hurled mock insults…"Your pigs are skinny, their plumes are pale and ragged." The choreography and explicit dialogue pointed out the relations between the sexes, usually resulting in the male looking foolish.

Cathy, remembering Robyn's explanations of the Bsorio battles of the sexes, thoroughly enjoyed the performances, laughing and scoffing right along with the natives.

The daily missionary skits, however, had even more effect on her. Early each morning the natives gathered in front of the Ellis hut for their daily "lesson." Marva and Pete, assisted by their children, acted out stories from the life of Christ, teaching the Bsorios graphically the simplicity of the Gospel message. Watching the daily tableau, the villagers set Jesus up as their hero, as they learned how He could do anything—heal the sick, raise the dead, feed the five thousand, give sight to the blind.

One morning Cathy woke early to an incredible sight. Though it was only seven, a magnificent full rainbow arched over the village, diffusing its violet-amber-green hues across a chocolate-colored sky. Pangs of memory stirred her emotions. Remembering that other rainbow over Harrowood, the one she had come to think of as hers and Robyn's alone, sadness swept over her.

Attempting to forget, she rushed to the Ellises, joining the numerous Bsorios who were also heading in that direction. An air of expectancy surrounded the village, perhaps because they had never seen a full rainbow before, or possibly because Pete had told them today's skit would be a special one.

Cathy sat in shocked horror with the Bsorios as they saw Jesus, their hero, beaten and crucified; she marveled with them as they saw Him rise again. Never had the gospel story had such an impact on her. When the story was completed, Marva and Pete explained over and over the simplicity of the Gospel—how believing that God's son, Jesus Christ, died in their place and

178

rose again would give them eternal life.

The village leader was the first to voice his faith. "I believe that Jesus died for my sins! I believe it!"

A young girl declared, "Before, Satan had me in his hand, but now Jesus has me in His hand!" Her face shone with God's peace.

Many others shared their faith in Christ, and some even clapped their hands for Jesus, praising Him for what He had done for them. Cathy's heart was heavy. She knew deep in her heart that the message was true. She desperately wanted the peace and joy the natives were experiencing, but it wasn't for her. It could never be for her.

She watched silently as Bate, wearing a mourner's mask of green mud, rose slowly to her feet. She held up her mangled left hand, revealing stubs where five fingers were missing. "To appease spirits, I cut off finger when I lost a child," she began. "I glad Jesus wiped slate for me! Before, my heart heavy, now light!" Cathy gazed in wonder as a beautiful smile broke through the sickly green mud, radiating across the woman's face.

Later, Cathy discussed the morning's events with Marva. "It must have been thrilling for you and Pete. I could almost see their lives changing before my eyes!" she exclaimed. "Especially Bate—I've never seen anything like it! Did she really cut off her own fingers?"

Marva nodded sadly. "It's a local custom. But she didn't tell the whole story. Each one of those five missing fingers represents a child she sacrificed to the alligator god."

Cathy sucked in her breath. "She killed her own babies? As much as she loves '*chilrun*'?"

"I'm afraid so. Another local custom."

"But this morning she looked so peaceful, so forgiven. God couldn't forgive murdering babies, could He?"

Marva stopped rolling out the bread dough and

picked up her Bible. "It says here that God forgives all sins. I don't see any exceptions, do you?"

Cathy eagerly read the passage she pointed out. "No, but..."

Marva flipped over to a passage in Isaiah. "Remember the verse Pete told you we had so much trouble translating?"

"The one about your sins being as scarlet, then being white as snow?"

"Right. Wouldn't that cover murder, too?"

Understanding and faith began to dawn in Cathy's long-burdened heart. "Can God forgive anything?" she whispered.

"He can and He will," Marva replied. "Why don't you ask Him to right now?"

A few moments later, a radiant, light-hearted Cathy rose from her knees, the burden lifted at last. "I feel so clean, so...so new!" she exclaimed. Like Bate said, 'Jesus wiped my slate clean!' "

Marva smiled radiantly. "Truly a rainbow of God's love and mercy arched over Bsorioland this morning, bringing brand new life to you and many of the villagers. I think this must be the happiest day of my life!"

Cathy hugged her. "This feeling of a great breakthrough—it is sort of like the rainbow after a storm, isn't it?"

"I think God has wrapped a rainbow of love around us all," Marva mused.

"I know exactly what you mean..." Cathy paused, a look of total wonder spreading over her face. "I don't even feel bitter against Chester. Can that be possible?"

Marva nodded. "Real life begins with Son-rise, when the Son of God enters our hearts and makes us new creations. Old things pass away, all things become new," Studying Cathy's face intently, she added, "Robyn will be delighted to hear about your decision.

Why don't you write and tell him?"

Robyn? Cathy hadn't thought about him at all during her newfound joy. Now at the mention of his name, the familiar longing surged through her like a flood. "Oh, I couldn't...I can't write to him...I think he's married."

Marva raised her eyebrows. "That's highly unlikely. I'm sure if Rob decided to get married, we would be among the first to know, and I haven't heard anything about any marriage."

A twinge of hope rose up in Cathy's breast. If he hadn't married Sylvia yet, maybe there was still a chance. On the other hand, if he had wanted her, he would have written or something. No word from him in five months surely didn't indicate a burning interest on his part. No, she wouldn't write to him.

"We'll be returning to the States in a couple of weeks," Cathy said quietly. "If you hear from Robyn again, you can tell him that I've found Christ." The words were spoken with a finality that clearly said the subject was closed.

But it wasn't closed in her heart. Rejoicing in her new life and fellowship with Christ, Cathy was amazed at how interesting the Bible had become. She devoured its pages, soaking in its truths. Yet the ache for Robyn was still there. Her love for Christ served to heighten her understanding of the kind of man Robyn was. How she missed him! How she yearned to share all the things she was learning with him!

She began teaching Bible stories to Heidi and Jed, as well as the Ellis children, and soon had most of the village children on her doorstep for storytime, a time she enjoyed as much as the children did.

One afternoon Heidi begged, "Will you teach us some funny stuff for Mom and Daddy before they come home?"

Cathy was puzzled by her earnest request. "Funny stuff?"

Heidi nodded. "Doesn't humor mean funny?"

"Yes, it does, but...."

"Those ten 'mandments you taught us say to humor thy father and thy mother, so I need some funny stuff!"

Cathy hugged her close. "That's honor thy father and thy mother," she corrected, trying hard not to laugh. *That's one I'll have to tell Robyn for sure*, she thought happily. "There I go again," she muttered aloud. "God, please help me to get him forever out of my mind," she prayed silently.

Chapter Fifteen

"Hurry, Aunt Cathy! Gotta surprise for you!" Heidi called from the door of the hut.

"I am hurrying, sweetheart. Just let me finish brushing my hair."

"Your hair sure looks pretty. I'm glad you let it down. Uncle Robyn's going to love…whoops!" She clasped her hand tightly over her mouth and drew back out the door, trying to halt the secret she had already let slip.

Cathy whirled around in alarm. "Robyn's coming here?"

"Correction," a male voice responded. "Robyn is here!"

After all these months, Cathy was dismayed to feel the same emotional tailspin at the sound of his voice. Unable to control her voice, she simply stared at him, a wide-eyed open message of love radiating from her face.

Robyn, too, seemed to have difficulty in speaking. Finally, he murmured huskily, "Don't I even deserve a hello?"

"It's…it's been so long," she stammered, still feeling very unsure of herself.

"Five months, two weeks, and four days, to be exact," he countered.

He hadn't cared enough to write, yet had kept an exact account of the time they had been apart. This man was an enigma. And just when she thought she had learned to face life without him, here he was back on her doorstep.

"You surely didn't think I would miss your farewell party, did you?" he asked.

"To be perfectly honest, I had no idea you knew anything about my party. How did you know we were leaving?"

"I've got friends in high places." He led her out to the porch where they could watch the party preparations. Two of the Bsorios were busily rotating the spit, roasting a wild pig over a fragrant wood fire pit. Marva and Pete were setting up long tables under the palms, giving orders to the children who were willing errand-runners.

"Actually," Robyn confessed, "the company sent me back up here for a few days of trouble-shooting on a piece of equipment at the mine, and Marva invited me to the farewell party."

"Oh." Cathy's face fell. So he hadn't come back to see her at all. His being here was simply coincidence. Her eyes lost some of their sparkle. "I'm glad you came. I didn't think I'd ever see you again."

His eyes blazed into hers, sending heat sweeping through her body. Finally, he spoke, his words coming in a hoarse whisper. "How I've missed you!"

She looked at him eagerly, her green eyes shimmering. "Why didn't you write?"

"I wanted to so many times, but with Dad's heart surgery in Sydney, things have been pretty hectic."

"Heart surgery?"

He drew back and gave her a puzzled frown. "You didn't know? You said Sylvia told you about it."

It was her turn to look puzzled. "She told me you were returning to Harrowood, but I had no idea it was because Matt was ill. How is he?"

He grew thoughtful. "Dad's doing fairly well, but he's still not up to full-time sheep operations. We could sure use your expertise. Do you have to return to the States? Why not come back to Harrowood as an employee?"

His rapid-fire questions intrigued and dismayed her at the same time. She would give anything to return to Harrowood—but as an employee? Carefully, she weighed her answer. Apparently he hadn't married Sylvia yet. Working with him every day might still give her a chance to win his love.

"All right. I'll go with you."

His face betrayed nothing. "Great. I know the folks will appreciate your help. Now, shall we join your party?"

They strolled out to the barbecue pit, where Heidi already had barbecue sauce smeared all over her face.

Robyn cupped her chin in his hands. "That face looks like a tablecloth after a spaghetti festival," he teased.

Heidi giggled. "Pasghetti festival?"

He winked at Cathy, just like old times. "I see you haven't taught her anything yet!"

"Rob, give me a hand with this tub of punch," Marva called. Cathy was delegated to pulling some of the children on their banana leaf sled.

A few minutes later, Robyn rushed back to her. "Do you think Bonnie and Joel could stay over a few extra days? I'd like Heidi and Jed to be in my wedding."

Cathy's heart lurched sickeningly, settling like a lead weight in her chest. "Your wedding?"

He beamed. "The woman I love accepted Christ recently, and I want to marry her as soon as possible."

Words couldn't get past the lump in her throat. Apparently Sylvia had become a Christian. Go back to Harrowood and see them together every day? Cathy knew she couldn't do it.

Pain dulled her eyes. "Robyn, I've reconsidered. I

185

can't possibly go to Australia with you. I can't go through with it."

"Can't go through with it! Why not?"

Swallowing her pride, she answered with complete honesty, "Because I love you."

"I had more or less counted on that. So why won't you go with me?"

She was incredulous. "Don't you understand? I love you, and would do almost anything for you—but don't you think that's asking too much of me?"

He shook his head. "I can't figure you out. You went anywhere Bonnie asked—let them walk all over you—out of love for Heidi and Jed. Do you love me any less?"

Was he suggesting that she do the same for him, despite his marriage to Sylvia? Refusing to let him see the enormity of her grief, she spun away from him, slamming into the house.

Robyn followed her inside, anger blazing from his eyes. "Before I leave here, I want one good reason why you won't marry me!"

She whirled around, facing him full on. "What did you say?"

"I said I want one good reason why you won't marry me!" he thundered.

"Marry you?" She groped for a chair, her legs too weak to hold her.

"Yes, marry me. Is that such a horrible idea?"

A brilliant smile flashed across her face. "I thought you meant marriage to Sylvia," she answered weakly.

"Sylvia? Why would I marry Sylvia when I'm toes over head in love with you?"

"But…I thought…she told me…."

"Sylvia and I had a long talk right after you left. I convinced her she didn't want to marry a sheep station, and she convinced me you loved me." He grinned broadly. "The last I heard she was in England—with a woolen mill merger in mind!"

Cathy laughed delightedly. "But what about Matt? Won't he be disappointed?"

"If he can't get Irish Echo in the bargain, I think he'll gladly settle for a sheep expert as a daughter-in-law!"

Suddenly, Cathy drew back. "I've got one more question. Why did you wait so long to ask me?"

He gave her a deep, searching look. "I couldn't believe you could care for me, even when Mother kept telling me you did. Then when I began to believe it, I knew I couldn't marry you, no matter how desperately I loved you, until you were a Christian."

He smiled ruefully. "That's why I pushed so hard to win you to Christ. I was afraid I'd break down and declare my love when I had no right. You can't know how hard I fought to keep from taking you in my arms, smothering you with kisses. Many times I had to keep my hands in my pockets just to keep from touching you."

He reached his arms around her, pulling her close. "When I realized you were going back to the States, getting you to work at Harrowood seemed like a good way to keep you nearby. Then when Marva told me a few minutes ago that you had accepted Christ, I wanted to take you to Harrowood as my wife!"

Her eyes wide with incredulity, Cathy turned in his arms and twined her arms about his neck. His hands cradled the back of her head as she brushed her lips softly across his. Robyn drew back. "Sorry, I can't kiss you!" he teased. "I'm a man of my word, and I promised never to kiss you again without an invitation."

Clinging to him in a sudden need to pour out her heart, Cathy whispered through half-parted, upturned lips, "If you can't recognize this as an invitation, I'm afraid there's no hope for you!"

Happily, they made plans to fly to Harrowood for the wedding. It would not take place until Bonnie and Joel stopped over in Australia on their return to the

States, so Heidi and Jed could take part in the wedding.

A few days later, their plane once again descended over a storm-washed Harrowood. "Look!" Cathy exclaimed. "There's our rainbow again!" Robyn dropped the plane down, as though planning to fly through the rainbow's multi-hued arch. "Our rainbow of promise," he murmured. "A promise that God's love and mercy will follow us all the days of our life together!"

Promise Romances™ are available at your local bookstore or may be ordered directly from the publisher by sending $2.25 plus 75¢ (postage and handling) to the publisher for each book ordered.

If you are interested in joining Promise Romance™ Home Subscription Service, please check the appropriate box on the order form. We will be glad to send you more information and a copy of *The Love Letter*, the Promise Romance™ newsletter.

Send to: Etta Wilson
P. O. Box 141000
Nelson Place at Elm Hill Pike
Nashville, TN 37214-1000

OTHER PROMISE ROMANCES
YOU WILL ENJOY

$2.25 each

Dear Reader:

I am committed to bringing you the kind of romantic novels you want to read. Please fill out the brief questionnaire below so we will know what you like most in Promise Romances™.

Mail to: Etta Wilson
Thomas Nelson Publishers
P.O. Box 141000
Nashville, Tenn. 37214

1. Why did you buy this Promise Romance™?

  ☐ Author   ☐ Recommendation
  ☐ Back cover description   from others
  ☐ Christian story   ☐ Title
  ☐ Cover art   ☐ Other_____

2. What did you like best about this book?

  ☐ Heroine   ☐ Setting
  ☐ Hero   ☐ Story line
  ☐ Christian elements ☐ Secondary characters

3. Where did you buy this book?

  ☐ Christian bookstore ☐ General bookstore
  ☐ Supermarket   ☐ Home subscription
  ☐ Drugstore   ☐ Other (specify)_____

4. Are you interested in buying other Promise Romances™?

   ☐ Very interested ☐ Somewhat interested
   ☐ Not interested

5. Please indicate your age group.
   ☐ Under 18 ☐ 25-34
   ☐ 18-24   ☐ 35-49 ☐ Over 50

6. Comments or suggestions?

7. Would you like to receive a free copy of the Promise Romance™ newsletter? If so, please fill in your name and address.

Name _____

Address _____

City _____ State _____ Zip _____

7362-5